USA TODA

V. Vee

A Very
Alpha
Christmas

His
Comfort &
Joy

He left to serve & protect his country.
He returned to serve & protect her.

His

Comfort &

Joy

A Very Alpha Christmas
(A For The Love Of The Marines
Novella)

USA TODAY Bestselling Author

V. Vee

HIS COMFORT & *Joy*

He left to serve and protect his country.
He returned to serve and protect her.

In 2015, Logan Steele kissed his girlfriend, Parker Leon,
goodbye and went to serve in the United States Marine
Corps overseas. It was the hardest thing he'd ever done.
In 2019, he returned.

He's changed. Nightmares plague him. He's hardened. No
longer the big teddy bear she once knew, Logan is battle-
scarred and war weary. He has secrets; and danger
follows him. But he came back for his woman. The woman
he lost touch with. The woman he still loves.

The woman who is keeping a secret of her own.

This Christmas, Logan does as all alphas do. He claims
his woman, and he fights whatever threatens her.
Even if the threat comes from him.

*The Very Alpha Christmas Series does not have to be
read in order. Each book is a standalone. *

COPYRIGHT

DEDICATED TO

For Nugget and

Bow.

THANK YOU

Thank you, Siren Allen and Shani G. Dowdell for letting me be a part of this experience and for understanding when my ass kept forgetting about it.

Thank you, Sara and Jayne for allowing me to escape into my room so I can work.

Thank you, Reana Malori for being understanding.

Thank you, Wendy Whitehead and Michelle D. Jackson for always checking up on me.

This story is not as long as some of my others. That is because this is a Christmas novella. But while not every question will be answered, it has enough to satisfy you (I hope! -cue me nervously biting my nails-)

And while I, personally, do not celebrate Christmas, being Jewish and everything, let's hope I sprinkled enough Christmas details and Christmas cheer throughout the story to make you smile.

Happy Chanukah, Merry Christmas, Happy Kwanzaa, and Happy Holidays!

-V. Vee

LOGAN STEELE SAYS GOODBYE

Logan Steele
2015

I kissed my girlfriend, Parker Leon, goodbye, wiping away her tears with my fingers. I knew she was upset about my leaving, and I also knew she didn't fully understand why I'd chosen to serve in the United States Marine Corps, but it was something I simply had to do. I needed to serve my country, needed to do something, anything, to feel like I was somebody. Like I had a purpose. Parker had one. She was a principal at a local elementary school, she helped to mold and shape lives. My days were spent working at the lumber yard, and boxing for some extra cash.

I needed to contribute to my world more. Needed to prove that my father's words about me were untrue. I was not worthless. I was not pathetic. And I was not mooching off Parker and her adopted parents' money.

And though I know Parker doesn't believe me, enlisting in the USMC, and knowing I would probably be leaving her behind? It was the hardest thing I've ever done.

"Please don't forget about me," Parker whispered.

I shook my head and pressed a kiss against her forehead.

"That could never happen," I promised her. "Don't you know you're my heart? I could never forget about you."

Parker nodded, though she glanced away. The look broke my heart, but I had to go. I didn't have any more time to soothe her fears and worries.

"I'll be back, Parker," I told her. "I promise."

Logan Steele
2019

I was finally home. Finally, back where I belonged. I stared up at the house where Parker lived now. Christmas lights of red and green, interspersed with white, covered the outside. An inflatable Frosty the Snowman © that looked as if it had seen better days, sat outside as if keeping watch. But it was the appearance of Santa Clause keeping vigil with Mary, Joseph, the wise men, and the a few shepherds, over the baby Jesus that made me smile the hardest.

I'd been slightly annoyed when I'd discovered that Parker had moved out of our little apartment about a year after I left but hadn't sent me her new address. But seeing her home, and knowing she was just as much of a freak for Christmas as always eased a bit of the ache within me. Besides. It didn't matter if she hadn't sent me her new information. I'd gotten rank. Security Clearance. I knew people. So it was easy for me to find her.

Stalker? Maybe.

Possessive? You bet your ass.

Determined? No one more so than me.

I knew she wasn't married. I'd had someone watching her for days and they hadn't seen a man coming in or out of her home, as a matter of fact, she'd barely left herself, so I was fairly certain she was still single. Still *mine*.

And it wouldn't matter if she did have another man in the house with her.

Parker belonged to me.

And though I've changed, and nightmares plague me, that fact was still true.

The Marines had hardened me. I'd gone from being the big teddy bear Parker once loved to cuddle up with, to being battle-scarred and war weary. I had secrets I didn't have before; and danger following me everywhere I went.

I wouldn't have come here, come back to Parker, if I had any other choice, because I needed to keep her safe, but I needed her more. My woman. The woman I'd lost touch with after going on mission after mission. On battle after battle. To country after country.

But Parker was the woman I loved. Even after all these years.

And I was going to do whatever I had to do, to make sure that when I left Arlington after Christmas, she was right there with me. By my side. Where she belonged.

No matter what I had to do to make that happen.

CHAPTER ONE

LOGAN RETURNS

🍬 🍬 🍬 🍬

Parker Leon

2019

I heard the sound of the animated creatures, laughing and playing, causing all sorts of mischief, long before I opened my eyes. I also heard two little voices, giggling and whispering to each other, extremely close to me. I checked myself internally. Had I had enough sleep? Could I possibly sneak out another hour or two before they realized that I was still alive and hopped on me to wake me up.

Most importantly: *Had I set the coffee maker's alarm to automatically make my big cup of the good stuff or would I have to be cognizant enough to do it myself?*

"Mommy? We know you're awake," my daughter Noelle's voice, innocent and yet firm in its childishness, made me smile.

"No, I'm not," I teased.

"Yes you are, Mommy!" Holly, Noelle's identical twin sister — and the other love of my life — said as she poked my cheek.

I laughed before pushing myself up in the bed. I shoved my curls — which I hadn't had years ago, but which had sprouted and grown in abundance when I was pregnant with the girls — out of my face and released a deep exhale before I got in "Mommy Mindset." I opened my eyes and gave my two little girls a smile. They were three, almost four years old, and though they were well-behaved, so beautiful they made my chest hurt, and more intelligent than any child had a right to be, there was still two of them and only one of me.

It could have been two of you if you'd only mailed that letter. My subconscious liked to remind me, at the very least, fifteen times a day, that I was a single mother, and all alone in Arlington, Virginia, because I'd *chosen* to be. It wasn't because Logan had cut off all contact with me, or even stopped contacting me. No, *I had left him*. But it had been a conscious, well thought out, decision. One I thought was best for everyone involved. Logan had discovered his "purpose" in the military and I'd known he was never going to come back, the realization had caused me pain at the time, so much I hadn't been able to eat, were it not for the miracles growing within me, my reasons for living two months after he'd left.

Our daughters. Our Christmas babies: Noelle and Holly.

"Mommy? Why you so sad?" Noelle asked with a frown.

I shook my head and reached out a hand to run it over my little girl's head. "I'm not sad," I told her. "Mommy is just thinking."

"'Bout what?" Holly questioned, and I turned to her with a grin. It was just me and my girls against the world. I'd lost both of my parents in a tragic accident a year before. I'd officially become an orphan again. Remembering their deaths still caused my breath to catch in my chest sometimes. No one had been able to explain to me how two older, highly educated, affluent, well-known, and wealthy black people, who were great contributors to the community, had been found, their car sprayed with bullets, in one of the more dangerous neighborhoods in Richmond.

My parents never went to Richmond.

Their murders had left me with a hole in my heart, one that was also filled with confusion, but I was a single mother and couldn't dwell on it or give it as much attention as I wanted to. Not when I had two little girls who depended on me for everything.

"Just thinking about Grandma and Grandpa," I told them, giving them a small smile.

"I miss Grammy and Grampy," Holly said, climbing up into my lap and placing her head on my chest.

"Me too," Noelle replied as she also climbed up in my lap.

I wrapped my arms around my girls and placed a small kiss on each of their foreheads. "Me three."

We sat in silence for a long time until there was a firm knock on the door. My eyebrows lowered in confusion as I checked the time on the clock. It wasn't time for my friend, Rachel Bradley, to come over just yet. She was bringing her kids over for a play date and also so I could have some much-needed adult time. She was in town because her husband had a game against the Baltimore Ravens, and instead of her and the kids spending their days in B-More, she was going to visit our friend, Kyra McCarthy, and then make her way down to Virginia to spend some time with us.

But she wasn't supposed to be at my place until the next day.

I lifted my girls from my lap and placed them down on the bed, before I grabbed my robe, wrapped it around my body and made my way to the front door. I rolled my eyes when there was another knock. Someone was extremely anxious to get me to open the door.

Which made me all the more eager to make them wait.

I stood just in front of the red painted wooden panel and crossed my arms. Waiting. When there was another knock, this one harder than the ones previous, I growled softly beneath my breath.

"Parker? Open up please! Let me know you're okay," a male voice came from the other side and I frowned before flipping the lock and twisting the doorknob.

"Steven?" I gasped, staring up into the dark brown eyes of my co-worker, the vice-principal of the school where I worked

as principal, *Sojourner Truth Academy*.
"What's wrong?"

"I was coming by to bring you this
month's quarterly reports, when I noticed a
man sitting in a SUV across the street. He's
been watching your front door for at least
an hour, but he hasn't gotten out. I was a
little concerned, especially since it took you
so long to open your front door."

Steven looked agitated and usually I
would have waved him off, in an attempt to
alleviate his concerns, but I looked over his
shoulder and noticed the SUV parked
exactly where he said it would be. I
frowned, a feeling of unease building
within me. Who the hell was that? And why
were they watching me? I wasn't that
interesting. I was the principal at an
elementary school, a single mother, an
orphan…

No one wanted anything to do with me. I had no enemies. And there was nothing fascinating enough about me to make someone want to stalk me.

No one except Steven.

My vice-principal had been unnecessarily *intrigued* by me since the day he was hired at the school over two years ago. He dropped by unannounced more than once, tried to engage in conversation with my daughters—which was a big no, no unless I was there to monitor said conversation—and was constantly trying to play the role of "boyfriend," to me. Even going so far as to be upset when he found out I went on a date six months ago. The date had been a disaster, much to Steven's happiness, but it hadn't been the fault of the guy I'd gone out with. Tierney O'Brien was someone I'd met when he'd brought his niece up to the school to register her. I'd been slightly blown away by his stunning good looks. From his shoulder-length strawberry blond hair, blue eyes, thick, but neatly trimmed beard, very broad frame, and tattoos running along the side of his neck and on both forearms that I could see, Tierney was nothing like the man I'd given my heart to. While Logan had tattoos, and a goatee, he hadn't been as broad as Tierney.

At least not when he'd left for the Marines. There was no telling what he looked like now.

Tierney had been the perfect gentleman on our date, so I'd been extremely disappointed that there had been no… *spark*. On either of our parts. He apologized to me as well, but while we wouldn't work as a romantic couple, we'd stayed friends. He often contacted me from Baltimore, or wherever else he was when he traveled for work, to check on me. And whenever he came to visit his sister and niece he stopped by. My daughters loved him and often asked me why he couldn't be their father.

But how did I explain desire, passion, lust, and love when I was still hung up on the man who'd left me to go and serve in some ridiculous war and hadn't returned?

You didn't contact him either.

Damn, my subconscious was being super persistent about that little detail today.

I reached out to pat Steven's arm. "Don't worry about it. It's probably just someone who is interested in buying the house." I pointed to the FOR SALE sign in my yard. "Remember, I'm selling?" I shrugged. "No doubt it's just someone who's interested enough to check out the house, but no interested enough to come knock on the door. No need to be concerned. Now…" I exhaled, having sufficiently calmed Steven's—and my own—trepidation. "What quarterly reports are you bringing me that couldn't wait for Monday? You know, when we return to work for our last week just before the Christmas break?"

Steven flushed and rubbed the back of his neck. "Oh, um… these." He handed me the stack of manila folders from inside of his messenger bag. "I just wanted you to have them as soon as I finished with them and um… you know, to check on you and the girls."

I laughed. "Steven, it's okay. I know. The girls and I are okay. I appreciate you always coming by to see about us, but it's really not necessary. And as for these?" I lifted the folders and opened my mouth to continue but the words froze in my chest when the driver's side door on the SUV opened and a man—a very large, bulky, older than I remember, *gorgeous*, man stepped from within, and closed it behind him once he had risen to his very tall height of six foot five if I remembered it correctly.

I gasped and shook my head, almost positive that my mind was playing tricks on me.

"Parker? Parker? Are you okay?" I could hear Steven asking me a question, but it came to me in a fog. I couldn't focus on him, not when the man from the SUV, a veritable *blast from the past*, came walking towards me, us, *me*, where we stood in the doorway.

When he stopped at the foot of the stairs and smirked at me, I finally found my voice.

"L-Logan?" I questioned breathlessly, not sure if he was actually there or if I'd conjured him from my fanciful musings. From my heartbreak and loneliness.

"Hey baby. Miss me?"

I couldn't even respond. Instead, I covered my face and burst into tears.

CHAPTER TWO

PARKER AND THE VICE-PRINCIPAL

Logan Steele
2019

I'd sat in my car for as long as I could.

Watching.

Furious. With rage boiling and swirling in my veins.

I'd watched as the tall, surprisingly muscled and toned, Asian man with black hair resting against his shoulders, stared at me suspiciously before marching up to the front door of my Parker's home and knocking. I knew he'd been just as curious about me as I was about him. I mean, fuck, the man had stood on the sidewalk in front of the house for about fifteen minutes before he'd finally noticed me. Then he'd walked up and down the street for another fifteen, before eventually going to no doubt warn Parker about the man sitting in his car, unmoving, unfazed.

But that wasn't the entire truth. While the idiot who thought it was his place to tell my woman *any-fucking-thing* seemed agitated by the mere possibility of my presence, I was already deciding what to do about him.

I wonder which one will cause him more pain. Removing his fingers, then his toes, then his arms, legs, dick, and then his heart, or perhaps just shooting him right in between the eyes? I mean it is the Christmas season. I should be charitable.

I would have stayed right where I was in my SUV and waited for him to leave, if only Parker hadn't… touched him.

My woman had her fucking hand on another man.

That was a big no-no. She was putting that man's life in danger just by smiling at him. But touching him? She was putting his family's lives on the line now.

While I wasn't as bad as my friend, Kynan McCarthy, however. Not when it came to the woman who breathed life into my soul. Oh no, Kynan who'd originally been called "Irish" by the rest of the Devils — brothers-in-arms, who serve in the Marines — in our platoon. He'd only been called that twice before he'd hemmed up one of the guys calling him that. The rest of us had stood around in surprise as he snarled in the other man's face like an animal, his lips pulled back, exposing his teeth, his green eyes flashing with green fire, and the red hair on his head — which had been cut down to be uniform, which was SOP: Standard Operating Practice, had shined like flames atop his head.

None of us even dared to step close to him. We were all called "Devils" or at least it was what some of us called each other, and yet, Kynan was the only one I could think of who actually legitimized the term. He looked and acted *exactly* as if he'd just crawled up from the depths of hell. His eyes were always flickering around the room, not in the same way the rest of us did… no, Kynan acted as if he were running *from* something, or waiting *for* someone. None of us knew exactly what it was, we just knew he was scary as fuck.

Which was why he and I had become fast friends. Most of the guys thought I was a little unhinged as well.

I'd been the only one to step close to Kynan that day, to try and dislodge his grip from its position around our fellow Devil's neck. Which was why I'd been close enough to hear what he'd said.

"Don't you ever call me that name again. If you knew the real *Irishman*, you would be quaking in your fucking coframes, with your little ass pack flooded with your piss, just *thinking* his name, much less saying it. You know my goddamn name. So say it properly or you and I will have to have this conversation in a totally different way. Got me?"

Then before I could reach out to grab him, Kynan had punch the wall, creating a hole where his fist had been, and I winced along with the rest of our brothers when he pulled his hand back and it was covered in blood. Kynan hadn't appeared as if he even felt the wound or the damage to his hand, but knowing I needed to get him away from everyone in the barracks before he did something even more foolish, I'd shoved him out the door to the nurse.

Kynan was a loose cannon, we'd all known that, which had made him perfect for the MOS we had. I never thought he would calm down or fuck, even smile, then he *FaceTime*™ me one day, a big, bright grin on his face and said three words to me.

"I found her."

I frowned at the huge smile on Kynan's face and shook my head as I walked out of the tent where I'd been camping out with a few of our other brothers. I was confused. Had Kynan been looking for someone? And if he were, why hadn't he told the rest of us so we could have helped him?

"Found who?" I asked.

Kynan chuckled—something else I'd never heard from him—and tugged a woman into the view of the camera as well. She wasn't as tall as my friend, but I could still tell she was not petite, either. Her skin was a sepia brown color, not as dark as my Parker's but not as light as that one singer everyone went crazy over... what was her name? Oh yeah, Beyoncé. Kynan's woman had eyes that were slanted and tilted up at the corners, like thin almonds. She had what Parker used to call, "bedroom eyes", so I could very much see why my friend had been hooked on her. Add her curvy frame— at least from what I could see in the camera's frame—and her hair which was in a high ponytail and if I hadn't been hopelessly in love with Parker, I may have just tried to take her away from my friend. Whoever she was.

"Ava meet my brother, Logan. We served together," Kynan introduced us. "Logan, this is my woman, Ava."

Ava, the woman Kynan had plastered to his side rolled her eyes. "I haven't agreed to be yours, Ky."

Kynan growled. "You agreed when you let me between your thighs, Brown Sugar."

"Kynan!" Ava gasped and I laughed, shaking my head.

"You must give him a run for his money, Miss Ava. I haven't seen Kynan with a woman since Afghanistan," I told her. "And if he's claimed you, he's not letting another man get near you."

Kynan's eyes narrowed. "You got that fucking right. I'd dismember any man that tried."

And I knew exactly how he felt. When I saw Parker's hand settle on the strange man's arm, my vision went red. I climbed out of my SUV with one thought in my mind.

Claim what's mine.

Which was why I walked straight up to where they stood. Her in the doorway of her home and him, outside, glancing over his shoulder at me. I knew the moment Parker saw me. Her eyes lit up with joy, then darkened with uncertainty, confusion, before finally pain and tears flooded those dark brown orbs.

My woman should never be in pain. Especially not because of me.

"L-Logan?"

I smirked at the man who stood in front of her, attempting to protect her from me.

Dumbass motherfucker.

"Hey, baby. Miss me?" I asked.

I was stunned when instead of answering me, she covered her face and burst into tears.

The man, whose name I still did not know—and that pissed me off more than anything—went to reach out to comfort her but stopped when I growled at him. Moving past him, I gathered Parker into my arms.

"Sshh. Baby. It's okay. I'm here now," I soothed her.

She shoved me away from her, or at least she tried to. Now that I had her back in my arms, I wasn't ever going to let her go again.

"W-What are you doing here?" she asked, wiping her face.

I shook my head and chuckled at her ridiculous question. She knew why I was there. She had to know. She was mine. I always came back for what belonged to me.

"I told you I was coming back for you," I told her. "Didn't you believe me?"

The tears in her eyes was all the answer I needed. She shook her head and wiggled in my embrace, attempting to get free. It was only the asshole behind me, clearing his throat that finally made me let her go, only to turn and face him, with my arms folded across my chest.

"Who the fuck are you?" I asked with anger tinging my words.

"Um… Logan this is Steven, my colleague. He's the vice principal at SJA. Steven this is Logan. My…"

"Her man," I answered, not appreciating the way Parker hesitated over who I was to her. I could see that she needed a reminder, and if the way my cock had hardened in my jeans was any indication, I couldn't wait to give it to her.

"I thought you were single, Parker?" *Steven* questioned with a frown.

I glared at him. "You were mistaken."

Parker shoved at my back and stepped around me. "No, he wasn't," she said shaking her head. "I *am* single."

"What the fuck, Park?" I growled.

She whirled around, her hair swirling around her shoulders before she poked me in the center of my chest.

"Four. Years, Logan. Four *fucking* years," she hissed. "I haven't seen you in *four motherfucking years.* You bet your ass I'm single."

I grinned at the way she sounded when she cussed. Parker was too… wholesome for the filthy words she'd just spewed at me, and yet, hearing them fall from her lips turned me the fuck on. I'd always made her use dirty words when we were together, and though her dark skin didn't completely show it, I always knew she blushed whenever she would say things like: "Fuck me, daddy," or "Lick my pussy, Lo."

Fuck. I couldn't wait to hear her say that again.

"It's Christmas, baby," I told her. "Of course I came home."

Parker shook her head. "Don't give me that bull, Logan. You've missed three Christmases. Almost four. What makes this one so special?"

I rubbed the back of my neck at the guilt that slithered through me at her words. She was right, of course, I'd missed plenty of Christmases, so why was this one so special?

I knew why, but damn if I wanted to tell her.

"I couldn't stay away from you. I've been overseas working and serving our country, and one day I looked around and realized that while I'd accomplished what I'd wanted to, it didn't mean anything if I didn't have you by my side, or waiting at home for me to return. Nothing matters without you."

Her eyes filled with tears again and she shook her head.

"When did you become so… poetic?" she wondered aloud.

I laughed. "When I was talking to the therapist they assigned me, and she asked me why I felt so unfulfilled." I shrugged. "The only answer I had was that I missed you. Your scent, your touch, your kiss. Everything. I needed you… I *need* you."

Parker waved her hands in the air. "No. No. Absolutely not. I'm not letting you back into my life that easily."

I chuckled. "Woman, you belong to me. And I came here not just for Christmas but for good."

She narrowed her eyes at me and looked me up and down. I knew what she saw. My body had bulked up, hardened, and tanned from my time in the Marines. I was tougher than I had been. I was more driven. More determined. I looked more like a lion than a bear. Even my hair had grown longer in the time I'd left the base and went on a journey to find her. And why she wasn't in our old place I would have to ask her. I liked her new home, but it seemed entirely too big for just the two of us.

"So, you're back just in time for Christmas, hmm?"

I nodded, once again gathering her close in my arms.

"Soo… Did you get me something or are you supposed to be my gift?" she asked with a watery smile.

"I did indeed get you a present," I whispered against her neck as I tugged her closer, pressing my thickening cock against her plush, soft body. She seemed… softer somehow. Her breasts were bigger, her hips rounder than they had been, and while she wasn't "fat", my girl definitely had put on some weight and there was a lot more for me to grab onto. She was "thick" now… and I loved it more than I could possibly put into words.

I could really fuck her and not have to worry about breaking her, I thought to myself.

"Well… I got one for you too. I've had it for about 3 years now." Parker looked at me hesitantly and for some reason, the expression on her face made me tense up. However, before I could question her about it, a small voice spoke from inside the house.

"Mommy? Who's that?"

I turned and looked down and saw a small girl... standing beside her twin... both looking up at me. I shifted my gaze to Parker, who looked guilty, and back to the little version of herself. They looked to be about three, maybe four... no, they had to be three, Parker had her period the month before I shipped out. Nine months of pregnancy and...

I quickly did the math in my head, before returning my attention to Parker.

"Holly? Noelle? This is Logan... your father," she answered the little girl, her eyes staying trained on my face.

I opened my mouth to respond but darkness swamped my vision and I knew nothing.

CHAPTER THREE

LOGAN AND THE STAKE OUT

2019

Parker Leon

He was outside my door again.

After passing out on my front porch, Logan had been dead to the world as Steven, the girls, and I tried to revive him. We'd finally gotten him inside and, on the couch, but while I was talking to my daughters, trying to explain why their father was only *just now* coming to our home, Logan had awakened, and left. Without a word of goodbye.

Again.

Then he'd shown up the next morning and sat outside in his SUV. I'd watched him and the girls had asked me over and over again why their "daddy" wouldn't come inside, but I hadn't known what to say.

How do I explain to them that whenever Logan got angry with me, he would leave, but keep me in his eyesight at the same time?

There had been one particularly bad argument, when he'd stomped out of our bedroom, only to grab a chair and follow me around the apartment, sitting no further than twenty feet away from me. Silent. Watching me with a mutinous expression on his face.

It always made me feel guilty.

But it also made me feel loved. As if he were saying—without words—that he didn't want to talk to me, but that he couldn't not be around me either.

Well, that's how he'd been before he'd enlisted of course. Then he was able to be away from me for four whole years.

That doesn't excuse you not telling him about his children, my subconscious reprimanded me.

If it wasn't bad enough that Logan was mad at me, and my daughters kept asking questions, and Steven kept sending text messages interrogating me about the man who was the father to my children whom he'd assumed was dead or not in the picture; my subconscious had been going nonstop with the snarky, angry, guilt-inducing commentary since Logan passed out in front of my home.

God! I wish he would just come in!

I huffed out a breath and jerked the curtain closed. I would go out to him, but remembering past arguments, that always made things worse. I was just going to have to wait him out, and hope he eventually decided to talk to me.

When there was a knock on the door, a firm, almost angry knock, I sighed in relief.

"It's about damn time," I said as I hurried to open the door. I jerked it wide and gasped when Logan stormed in, picking me up in his arms and turning to pin me against the wall.

"You kept my fucking children away from me for three years?" He snarled.

"You left me!" I accused him right back.

"I was *working*!"

"You were *running!*" I growled in his face. When he blinked at me, I poked him in the forehead. "You took off because of what my father and your father said to you. Your father told you that you would never amount to anything. That you would always be mooching off my family and you were pathetic, and when my father asked you what your intentions were and if you could provide for me and our future family, you got scared! You took off. This had absolutely *nothing* to do with you wanting to serve this damn country."

"Parker..." he shook his head.

"Fuck this damn country!" I yelled at him. "And fuck you too! You *left* me. You were willing to give us up for your goddamn pride. And when you sent me that letter telling me you were thinking about doing eight years instead of four?" I swung my head side to side. "I knew you weren't coming back. I knew that was your way of telling me to sit around with my thumb up my ass while you *found* yourself."

I inhaled deeply, tears coming to my eyes. "But I couldn't wait, Logan. I was pregnant. And I was going to tell you until you said that to me. And then… I just… I didn't. Because you didn't deserve to know them, and you didn't deserve me."

And like that, as if all the air had been let out of his body, Logan set me back on the floor and took a few steps away from me.

"Is that what you thought?" he asked, sadness darkening his eyes.

"It's what I know," I replied.

"Mommy? Are you fighting with Daddy?" Noelle's voice pierced the haze of my fury, frustration, and despair. I turned to her and pasted a smile on my face.

"No honey!" I lied. "Sometimes adults just talk really loud when they're happy to see each other."

Noelle just stared at me for a long moment, not saying a word, before she looked back at Logan.

"You're my Daddy?" she asked.

Logan swallowed and nodded. "I am."

Noelle just watched him, silently, before she spun on her heel and walked away.

"Fuck. That was worse than uniform inspection," he muttered.

I snorted out a laugh and made a move to follow my daughters. I knew if Noelle was coming out to check on me, then it wouldn't be too long before Holly would make her way down the hall to simply stare at me. I gasped when Logan grabbed my arm, swinging me around to face him again.

"We're not done, Park," he said, his eyebrows low on his face, a frown pulling his lips down.

"Yes." I snatched my arm out of his grip. "We are."

Logan shook his head and pointed down the hallway where Noelle had just walked down.

"Those are my daughters, but they don't know who I am. They don't know how to feel about me. They don't know whether I'm a good guy or a bad guy." He ran his fingers through his hair, and my eyes followed the movement. I could remember him, resting his head in my lap, and my own fingers caressing the soft strands as I lulled him to sleep.

"What do you want me to do about it?" I questioned, my hands on my hips.

Logan looked at me as if I'd just asked the stupidest question in the world, and I guess, in a way, I had. I rolled my eyes and tossed my hands up in the air.

"Fine, Logan! Fine!" I sighed then turned towards the bedrooms. "Holly? Noelle? Can you come here please?" I waited for the sound of their little feet padding down the hall. Once they'd reached us, I walked over to them and knelt down in front of my two girls before looking over my shoulder at Logan.

"Remember how I told you that Logan was your father?" I asked them.

Holly and Noelle nodded, looking uncertainly at the man who had helped to create them.

"Well, he wanted to meet you. What do think of that?"

I watched as both girls looked at each other, having a quiet twin conversation, before returning their gazes back to me.

"Okay, Mommy," Holly said.

I nodded then rose to my feet and stepped behind my daughters in order to present them to their father.

"Holly, Noelle, this is your father, Logan. Logan, your daughters: Holly and Noelle."

Logan stepped forward and crouched down in front of them. "It's nice to meet you both." He swallowed and guilt tumbled through my belly at the sight of tears filling his eyes. "You're both so beautiful."

"Thank you," they said simultaneously.

We all stood in silence for a minute before Noelle spoke up.

"Daddy?"

Logan cleared his throat and nodded. "Yes, love?"

"Why didn't you want us?"

Chapter Four

Stacey, Gregory, and The Truth

Logan Steele
2019

I stared at my daughters in awe and wonder.

They were little mixtures of both Parker and me. With skin the color of birchwood, light brown curls that fell down their backs, big hazel eyes, and identical expressions of hesitation and fear on their faces, I couldn't believe I'd helped to create them. I wish I'd had the opportunity to be there with them from the moment they'd been born, but I'd been denied the opportunity.

Because you chose to stay away, my subconscious reminded me.

Man, the truth could be a bitch sometimes.

Parker and I had attempted to explain to Noelle and Holly why I was just meeting them. That I didn't know they existed. Because I was off fighting bad guys in another country. That I loved them already. But I wasn't so sure if they understood or accepted our explanation.

And that just pissed me off even more than I already was.

I punched the hanging punching bag in front of me repeatedly, getting lost in the rhythm of my gloved fists hitting the weighted material over and over again. I was venting my frustration over the entire situation.

Parker saying she was single.

The fact that I was a father.

Parker's co-worker, Steven, thinking he had a fucking chance with *my* woman.

The fact that I was a father.

How my daughters didn't know me, and I didn't know them.

The fact that I was a father.

The motherfucking fact that I was a father.

"Whoa! Loge, what the fuck man? Are you trying to break my shit?" My best friend, Gregory Richmond, asked as he walked up to me on the other side of his home gym. I didn't usually come over to Greg's house to workout. The two of us most often met at another gym, *Gold's Gym™*, but ever since Greg and his wife — and *his* best friend — Stacey, had gotten married and had children, my best friend who was a man who'd formerly loved to do anything that kept him away from his place of residence, barely wanted to go more than fifteen feet from his front door.

He said it had to do with his "gut" telling him that he needed to be close, but we all knew it was because he was so fucking happy, he never wanted to leave them. Which made his personal security business very hard to run. Though he ran it with his wife, which made it just *slightly* easier.

"My bad, man," I apologized, stopping the bag and walking over to grab my towel to wipe away the sweat on my forehead.

"What the fuck is up with you, Loge?" Greg asked me.

I shrugged and went to walk past him to the refrigerator where he kept the bottles of water. I stopped when he reached out to grab my bicep. There were few people in my life who could match my size.

Kynan was one, and Gregory was the other. We were all big men and when the three of us used to go out to bars all of the women in the building flocked to us.

Gregory and I never entertained them, Kynan would take two or more home with him. Though I suspected he wouldn't be doing that anymore.

That should be me. I should be just as fucking happy as these two jackasses.

"I take it things didn't go so well with Parker?" Greg asked.

I snorted and shook my head.

"Oh, it went about as well as I expected," I told him. "She saw me, got angry, cried, then got angry again. That's not what's got me so fucked up in the head."

Greg frowned. "Then what the fuck is your deal, dude?"

I sighed and flopped down on the weight bench that rested against the wall.

"I'm a dad."

It was the first time I'd said the words to anyone other than myself, and the silence that greeted my statement let me know it was just as crazy, fucked up, and amazing as I suspected.

"What the hell do you mean you're a dad?" Greg asked.

"Exactly what the fuck I just said man. While I was overseas, Parker had my daughters. Two of them. Girls. Twins," I revealed, shaking my head.

"*Holy. Fucking. Hell.*"

"You can say that again."

"Holy. Fucking. Hell."

"Greg!" Stacey's shocked gasped made the both of us jump up from where we sat, apologizing not only to her, but also to the two little boys who stood in front of her, big grins on their faces.

"Mommy! Daddy said bad words!" One of them said with glee. I couldn't tell Greg and Stacey's boys apart, but my own little girls? I knew exactly which one was Holly and which was Noelle.

Holly had a little beauty mark next to her right eye and Noelle had one next to her mouth. My daughters were identical to everyone but her mother and me.

"Yes, he did," Stacey replied, her hands on her hips.

I chuckled when Greg's face flushed red.

"Sorry boys. Daddy won't say that again," Greg responded.

Stacey stepped into the room, following behind the boys: Shawn and George, as they headed over to a corner filled with tiny weights for kids. I shook my head as they both began to "workout" just like their father had been.

"So, what's going on that you felt you just *had* to use profanity in front of our children, Greg?" Stacey asked.

Greg jerked a thumb in my direction. "Loge just found out that his woman, Parker, had twin girls while he was overseas."

Stacey's eyes widened before she turned to look at me. I shifted uncomfortably as her gaze traveled up and down my body, taking in my worth. She shook her head.

"Don't tell me, you're mad at her?" She asked, crossing her arms.

"I mean… don't I have the right to be?" I questioned her.

Stacey shrugged. "Disappointed? Absolutely. Feeling as if you have been robbed? Oh yeah. But mad?" She shook her head. "You were the one who stayed away, Logan. When the rest of the guys took time to come home and visit their families over the years, you chose not to. Why?"

"Because…"

Stacey held up a hand. "No. Don't spout out the same…" she looked over her shoulder, "bull crap that you tell yourself, or Greg, and maybe even Parker, to try and justify your actions. You need to think long and hard about why you stayed away, and if maybe, just maybe, that's why you're really angry. Not because she didn't tell you, but because you know that if you'd come home you would have found out for yourself."

And for the first time since finding out about Noelle and Holly I stopped thinking about the secret Parker had kept from me and instead considered the reason I'd stayed away from the woman who was

the very beat of my heart. And when I
realized why it was, guilt and shame flowed
like sludge in my veins.

CHAPTER FIVE

LOGAN V.S. NOELLE & HOLLY

Parker

2019

I stood with hesitation at the
entrance of my living room, dressed in my
professional dark blue skirt suit, with a grey
button-down shirt, my hair twisted up into
a French knot at the back of my head, as I
watched Logan play with Noelle and Holly.
I wasn't exactly sure how I felt about
leaving my girls with him. I mean, yes, he
was their father, but he didn't exactly *know*
them.

And whose fault is that?

I shoved away the offending voice of my conscience and bit my lower lip as I considered my options.

I had a very important meeting at the school.

When Logan had shown up earlier in the day, we'd had a talk... okay, we'd had a shouting match, and come to the tenuous agreement that he would spend the day — maybe the next few days or weeks, getting to know the girls. But it would start today.

That was before I'd gotten the call.

The call from my assistant who was simply reminding me about the required quarter meeting with the teaching staff, in addition to the PTA meeting. Neither of which I could get out of. Both of which I had to attend. Which meant I had to send Logan home and get a babysitter.

At least, that had been my plan until I said those actual words to Logan. In front of our daughters.

I'd never been the enemy before. I tried to maintain a pleasant personality around everyone so that I was well-liked and universally loved, but the moment I told my girls their father had to leave because I had to go to work? Well...

I'd become the epitome of every villain of every princess in every storybook I'd ever read to them.

Damn Disney Princesses.

So, I'd... compromised, though Logan had said I'd conceded. I was going to allow Logan to watch the twins, but he had to send me a picture every hour, so I knew they were okay and still in my home.

And I didn't just mean Holly and Noelle.

Though Logan and I obviously had hurt feelings regarding each other, betrayals, misconceptions, lies, etc. to work through, the feelings I had been trying to deny for the man whom I had been in love with for so long, the man who'd given me my babies, began to resurface. I had tried to fight them off for as long as I could, but I felt helpless to stop them.

I was falling in love with Logan again.

Or maybe I'd never really stopped loving him.

"Alright guys! I'm leaving! Anyone going to come give me a hug and kiss goodbye?" I waited to be assaulted by my little girls, to feel their little bodies colliding with my own, to inhale their sweet, innocent scent. However, nothing happened for long moments. I looked around in confusion and repeated myself again.

"Bye Mommy!" The twins called out in tandem, neither of them coming to hug me, just before they burst into giggles over something their *Daddy* had said.

Didn't they know he was just going to hurt them? To leave them? To abandon them? That's what he did to the women he loved and the women he had call him: "Daddy."

I clicked my tongue in disgust and turned to leave.

"Where do you think you're going?"

Damn his voice. After all this time it still sent shivers down my spine.

Without even answering, I kept walking towards my front door.

"Don't be stupid, Logan. You know where I'm going," I tossed over my shoulder.

I gasped as he spun me around, his name on my lips, but he stole the breath from my lungs when he took my mouth in a hard, deep, punishing kiss. When he released me moments later, I blinked in surprise. Every brain cell I possessed had been fried, drowned, blown to smithereens and tossed into the biggest, most tumultuous ocean in the world.

No… the universe.

I heard his chuckle and shame soared through my veins.

C'mon bitch, don't give in so easily, I chastised myself.

"I knew you still wanted me," he said. "You can fight with me, argue with me, and deny it all you want to, but your nipples and the way you're panting give you away every, single, time." His eyes twinkled with mischief and had I not been trying to lead by example for my daughters, regarding physical violence against others, I would have pulled back my fist and socked him right in the eye.

Not wanting to give him the satisfaction of watching me as I checked the front of my button-down shirt to see if my breasts had also betrayed me, I spun on my heel and left, heading through the open doorway, out to my car, and straight to the school.

Where I finally glanced down at the curve in my button-down shirt where my tits lay.

Where my nipples still protruded against the fabric.

Damn.

I was trying to pay attention. I really was. But it was extremely difficult. Not when I knew *that man* was in *my* home and watching *my children*.

Okay, I know, they're his children also, but they were mine *first*.

And yes, I know, I sound like a spoiled brat.

I groaned silently and sat back in my leather chair, as Steven continued giving his presentation regarding violence in schools and our school's plan to combat it. It was the same presentation he'd been giving for the last few years. We all basically knew it by heart. And yet, Steven still insisted on delivering it. Even though the violence in our school had decreased from 60% down to 13%. It wasn't as low as I would have preferred it, but the school board was impressed. Which meant my job was safe.

My Apple Watch™ vibrated and when I glanced down my eyes widened at the number calling me. I gestured for Steven to continue as I hurried out of the room.

"Hello?"

"Hello? Is this Parker Logan?"

"Yes, this is she. May I ask who's calling?"

"Yes, ma'am. This is the Arlington Police Department. We were called out to your home due to a small fire that broke out in the home. Now, there's no need to be alarmed. It was put out quickly and no one was harmed, however…"

I took off running, not even bothering to say goodbye to my colleagues, or to finish listening to the officer on the phone. There had been a fire at my house, and I had to go and check on my family.

When I pulled up in front of my house the fire trucks had apparently already left since they were not in front of my home. There were, however, three police cars sitting outside, and six officers congregated in my yard. Two officers were playing with Noelle. Two were... coloring with Holly. And the other two appeared to be shooting the shit with Logan.

And was that a *dog* taking a shit in my yard?

I slammed my car door and raced up to the crowd that were clustered in my yard.

"Mommy!" My daughters yelled in unison as they ran towards me. I knelt before them; my arms outstretched. I gathered them closely to me, kissing their precious foreheads and checking them over for bruises, injuries, and burns. I didn't care what that officer said, a mother knew better than any emergency personnel or first responder if their child was injured.

Mine were not.

But I knew that *now*.

"Mommy! Daddy's new puppy knocked over the Christmas tree!" Holly said, her hazel eyes shining with excitement.

Logan bought a puppy?

"And then the puppy was fighting with some of the branches and tossed some of them into the fireplace!" Noelle continued with the story.

I closed my eyes in horror and guilt as soon as Noelle's words left her lips. I'd been meaning to clean the chimney and fireplace for a while now. Especially the flue. Steven had been warning me for a long time that if I didn't do it a fire would break out in my house.

I hated it when he was right.

I hated it even more that Logan and my girls had been in the house when it had happened.

"When did your daddy get a puppy?" I asked, returning to a key element of the girl's retelling.

"When the refused to eat their vegetables," Logan responded, and I turned towards him.

Though I wouldn't admit it at the time, my gaze traced over his form, checking for any visible signs of injury, pain, or burns. I didn't see any, so I returned my focus back to what he'd said. I frowned and shook my head.

"You bought the girls a puppy because they wouldn't eat their vegetables?" I wondered aloud for clarification.

Logan merely shrugged. "They wouldn't race against me in push-ups, so I had to find a better way."

I gestured to my home.

"And buying a new puppy and letting that dog destroy my home is how you get them to eat vegetables, Loge? Really?" I shook my head at him, feeling completely exasperated and frustrated.

"Hey. Don't get huffy with me. I didn't exactly know they turned into little terrors when you tried to get them to eat something *green*, you know, because you never *fucking told me they existed!*" He growled.

I pointed up into his face. "Don't you *dare* try to turn this around on me, Logan! You left. You never came back. You were planning to stay longer. You didn't *deserve* to know they existed! You didn't deserve them then, and you don't deserve them now."

I refused to step back as he bent down until our faces were practically touching.

"Them... or you, Parker?"

I narrowed my eyes at him, then taking the girls' hands in mine, I turned and marched back towards my smokeless, yet slightly charred home, ignoring their protests and cries for their "Daddy." Their *daddy* could rot in hell for all I cared.

And with that thought, I slammed the door shut.

Right in the faces of Logan and his damn vegetable dog.

CHAPTER SIX

LOGAN AND THE "KISS"

🍬 🍬 🍬 🍬

Logan Steele
2019

I was taking a huge risk with my life. I knew I was. Parker was no doubt still upset with me about the dog and the tiny little fire from the night before, but I wasn't going to let that stop me from being with her and my girls. Now that I had them back in my life, nothing was going to keep me from them.

I knocked on the front door and waited, my ears listening intently for the smallest sound coming from inside. I heard

Holly and Noelle's laughter, and Parker's huskier voice as she responded to them, the sound coming closer to the front door. I knew the minute she came up to the door and looked through the peephole. As always, my skin tingled from her gaze.

I needed her to open the door and let me in before my hard dick bore a hole through the wooden barrier.

Once the locks disengaged, I leaned against the doorway, pushing my dirty blond hair back from my forehead. I hooked leather, motorcycle jacket over my shoulder, making sure my thick biceps were on display and showing beneath my white t-shirt, jeans riding low on my hips, and wrapped snugly around my thick, tree trunk-like thighs, with my favorite motorcycle boots on my feet.

I watched as Parker's gaze moved over me and swallowed back the groan that threatened as her eyes darkened. There she was. My Parker. The one and only. The woman of my dreams. The woman who belonged to me. Who always had.

And always would

God, she looked amazing.

"L-Logan," she stammered out breathlessly. Parker was wearing a light pink tank top, with a pair of loose cotton, grey shorts riding low on her full hips. Her thick black hair was pulled up into a ponytail at the top of her head, her face clean and devoid of makeup, her full lips parted in surprise. Her dark brown skin was on display, and man, did I look and enjoy the view.

I couldn't wait to taste her again.

"Good morning, Gorgeous. Can I come in for a cup of coffee?" I asked, feeling my lips turn up into a sexy smirk when she simply continued staring.

"Umm… y-yes, come on in," Parker stammered and opened the door wider so I could step in.

I went to move past her but before I did, I leaned down to whisper a promise into her ear.

"I'm going to take you. Hard. Every inch of you. With my mouth, my tongue, my teeth, my fingers, my hard cock, and my seed. And after I cum, I'm going to take you again."

I heard her gasp in surprise, and I chuckled darkly before leaning down to press a chaste kiss on her lips. It had to be chaste and quick—the only time I did anything quick when it came to this woman—because if I had kissed her the way I wanted to, I would have lifted her up into my arms and fucked her against the wall.

Children and neighbors be damned.

And really, I wasn't that type of guy — usually — but it had been way too long since I'd felt the tight squeeze of Parker's slit around my aching cock and I was growing impatient.

I stepped into the living room where my girls were watching some show with a talking baby… talking babies — what the hell kind of cartoon was that? — and said hello to them, before settling down to spend time with them. I was distinctly aware of Parker entering the room long minutes later, her eyes bright and hard nipples pressing against the fabric of her shirt and I smirked again, knowing my words had affected her. Knowing that she'd probably taken a moment to rub her pussy and have an intense orgasm before reentering the room.

I watched her as she made her way over to the opposite couch, reaching out to snag her hand, her *left* hand, and brought it up to my mouth. I pressed a kiss to her palm and flicked my tongue over her fingers.

Fuck.

Just as I'd suspected, though she'd no doubt washed her hands, I could still fucking *taste* her on her slender fingertips.

She was still just as delicious as I remembered.

"Ew! They're kissing!" Noelle exclaimed.

I released Parker's hand and winked up at her, noticing that she was breathing much harder than before, and turned to my girls.

"You kiss people that you love. So, I'm going to kiss you now!" I said, and jumped up, stomping towards her like a monster.

"No!" Noelle screamed, a giant smile on her face. She grabbed Holly's hand and the two took off running. I gave chase, pausing long enough to smack Parker's ass, before I ran after my girls. Kissing them each on the cheeks, before letting them run off again.

I may not have known about them before. I may be new in their lives but that love, that connection was there. That need to protect them. To do anything to make them smile, make them laugh, make them happy was there as well. They were as important, if not more so, than their mother.

Which meant I had to clean up some loose ends from the time I spent in Germany before my bad decisions in the military came back to bite me in the ass.

🍬 🍬 🍬 🍬

Hours later, the girls were in bed and Parker and I were sitting in the same living room we'd been in earlier that day. We were talking. Or rather, Parker was babbling about her job, the girls, anything she could think of to try and ignore the tense, sexually charged atmosphere between us. I was going to give her more time to chatter on about nonsensical things, matters that could all be discussed in the morning, but the force of the surging need and lust inside of me, coursing through my veins had come to a breaking point, and I couldn't wait any longer. Parker and I belonged together, needed to be together.

Now.

"When was the last time you were with someone, Park?" I asked when there was a slight lull in the conversation.

The tip of her tongue appeared and swept the sensual curve of her bottom lip. She shifted on the overstuffed armchair she was sitting on. No doubt trying to get pressure on that pretty, fluttering clit. Attempting to ease the empty ache deep inside her that my words had caused.

Oh, my poor baby. Has it really been that long?

In a gesture that had to be unconscious, that was both seductive as hell and sweet, she brushed her fingers over her mouth. As if she were remembering something. A kiss. A tongue. Feeling the stretch of her lips around a cock.

My cock.

"Not since you left," she admitted.

"Have you wanted to sleep with another man?" I pressed, the question barely audible to my own ears through the filter of dark, thick lust pounding in my head, my body. I was angry at the thought of any man touching what belonged to me. Enraged at the thought that any other asshole had the opportunity to take what was mine. Or that Parker would want them to, but I remained in my seat. I needed to hear her answer. Before I proceeded, I needed to know if I were erasing some other fucking asshole from her memory, or if I were simply solidifying my place there.

"No," she whispered with hesitation. "You're the only man I've ever truly wanted to be with." She looked up at me, her eyes full of pain and devastation. The look ripped through me and I felt guilty.

Guilty because, hypocrite that I am, I'd slept with other women since Parker cut off communication with me. At least three. None of them were her, however, and though I'd tried to find women all over the world who reminded me of the only woman who possessed my heart. It had been difficult sometimes not only to find one, but to even get an erection. So often I'd had to close my eyes and imagine it was Parker's mouth sucking me dry. Her pussy I was pounding into. Her ass I was sliding in. Her screams assaulting my ears.

A shudder rippled through me; I was disgusted with myself that I hadn't been able to preserve myself for her. That I hadn't had more restraint. And yet...

Maybe Parker had the ability to peer beneath the quickly crumbling shields of my control, my guilt, and see the ever-present, always hungry need to get my hands on her, and the love I always had for her. It must be her secret power because only seconds later, she lowered herself from off the chair and sank to her knees in front of the couch where I was perched.

Right in between my legs.

"I wonder if you still taste as good as you used to," she whispered.

The last charred vestiges of my restraint and conscience screamed at me that while I'd begun this entire situation, that Parker and I still needed to talk. To clear the air, but I ignored them both and slid back on the couch until my spine hit the cushion, before I lowered my hands to my belt.

Unbuckled it.

Unfastened the button at the waist of my jeans and tugged down the zipper.

The movements were... deliberate.

A part of me was giving Parker a way out, but another part of me wanted her desperate for me. Aching for me.

I was trying to punish her for running from me. For not telling me about our daughters.

For thinking she could walk away from me.

But in trying to punish Parker — with her lips parted, her chest rising and falling as if struggling to drag in air — I am also putting myself in an agonizing, painful grip of lust. Reaching inside my boxer briefs, I fisted my erection. The rush of relief as I squeezed my throbbing, hard-as-hell flesh made me groan as if I were enduring hot rocks being placed against my naked skin. The sound scrabbling its way up my throat and rumbling out of me. Parker's pretty, dark brown eyes fixated on my pumping hand only increased the pleasure-with-a-bit-of-pain higher.

"Gimme," she whimpered. That goddamn whine stroked over me like an eager, warm tongue.

Hers.

It had been way too long since I'd experienced the wonder of her mouth. The utterly delectable stroke of her wet tongue stroking the stalk of my dick. I shoved the cotton and denim down, needing her to see all of me is just as she remembered. Just as hard for her. Just as aching.

I needed her to crave me with the same gnawing, unyielding greed that had been plaguing me for years. I stroked my fist over my length, slower, harder, feeling oddly dissatisfied, because no one could handle my cock like Parker. How could I fuck my hand with this goddess of a woman right in front of me? This woman who knew just how I liked it? But I was trying to prove a point.

Though if it was to her or myself, I'd completely lost sight of.

Short, harsh pants punctuated the air like small blasts, though I wasn't sure if they were Parker's or my own. Her gaze flicked from my face to my dick, back to my face, then down again. Like she couldn't decide which to stare at — couldn't decide which she enjoyed watching more. If I had her spread wide on the couch, shorts, tank top, and underwear gone, I might have had the same dilemma.

Who am I trying to kid? No, I wouldn't have.

Parker was gorgeous. Her face could stop traffic during rush hour. But her naked, wet, swollen folds... Yeah, that pussy would either cause a damn riot or start a fucking war.

Damn.

I closed my eyes at the image of what she looked like vulnerable and exposed, offering that perfect sex to be claimed, corrupted, branded, and licked my lips. Another groan rolled out of me as I enclose the tip of my cock in my hand, twisting.

"C'mere, Parker," I beckoned, curling the fingers of the hand not wrapped around my dick around the back of her head. "Touch me."

Her long, elegant fingers pressed down on my jean-covered thighs, and the muscles involuntarily contracted under her palms. *Goddamn*, I could have come just from that light touch. Clenching my jaw, I stared down at her, part of me reeling in surprise. After years of going without this woman's touch she was back before me, kneeling before me, hunger darkening her gaze, her hands and mouth inches from my dick.

"What do you want?" I asked her, burrowing my hand in her hair. The thick, heavy strands slid over my palm, in between my fingers, and my imagination ran amok. That dark hair gliding over my bare skin. Wrapped around my dick. My grip tightened at the vivid, dirty visuals, and Parker inhaled sharply. Her lashes fluttered, and a small whimper echoed between us.

I hardened even more at her obvious signs of pleasure. And just because I could, I twisted her hair around my hand, tugging again at her scalp. With another of those sweet, utterly sexy sounds, she leaned into my hold.

God, I forgot how fucking perfect she was. How could I have forgotten?

"Tell me, Parker."

"I want you. In my mouth. Your hand in my hair. Guiding me. Taking what you need from me," she said, her fingers curled into my thighs. "Don't be gentle. Use me. I want to feel like a *woman*. Not like a principal. Not like a mother." She looked up at me and I felt as if I'd been punched right in the sternum, I was blown away by the dark desire I could see in her eyes. "I want to feel like *your woman* again."

Her words crashed into one another the longer she spoke, as if they were as surprised as I was by what she was saying that they didn't know which way to go, which way to turn. But it didn't matter; I heard every syllable and I knew *exactly* where to go.

Breathe, motherfucker.

Inhale. Exhale. Inhale. Exhale.

My control slipped away more and more with each breath, like delicate tissue paper that was steadily tearing right down the middle. Only Parker could do this to me with just a whispered plea.

I rubbed my thumb across her bottom lip, tracing the curve, dipping the tip inside. The edge of her teeth grazed my flesh, and the sensation rippled over my erection. Anticipation rode me hard, drumming deep inside me, sizzling under my skin. A part of me wanted to hold out a little longer, but damn that. I couldn't. Not when I'd been without this woman for years.

Taking what you need… Don't go easy… Use me.

The litany played in my head, a filthy little jingle that quickly became my favorite tune. I wrapped my fingers around the bottom half of my length again, and tugged her head down, down, down, until…

Oh fuck.

Her lips kissed the head of my cock for a chest-squeezing moment before they parted, opened, and I was sinking into the wet heat of her mouth. My body went as rigid as a statue. *Christ.* Our moans saturated the air, and as hers vibrated over my flesh, I can fully believe that Parker had been waiting for this — wanting this — for years. Waiting for me to come back. Wanting me for as long as I have been aching and dying for her. With my dick encased in the sweetest suction imaginable, I don't have to picture her any longer, or the feel of her body underneath my hands.

Just as always, Parker didn't wait for me to instruct her; her tongue slid over the swollen tip, smoothing, exploring. I didn't stop her. That would have required moving. And I was paralyzed by such sharp pain-edged pleasure, I was a willing prisoner of her mouth.

She dipped her head, taking more of me, that agile tongue torturing me with its long, greedy strokes. Only when she withdrew, and the cool air whispered over my damp skin did my stupor shatter. With a growl that sounded just a little too damn animalistic, I pressed her head lower, not easing until her lips bumped my fist. I knew she could take it, and I was going to make sure she remembered that fact.

Shit.

The sight of her mouth stretched wide around my dick... No fantasy, no porno, no part of my current reality could compare to it. The way she eagerly worked her tongue, the slight flush across her dark cheekbones, the bite of her nails through the denim of my jeans telegraphed her pleasure to my lust-soaked brain. Then there were the moans adding another caress up and down my flesh. It was so fucking good. I couldn't tear my gaze away from her. Couldn't believe I'd gone years without her. Watching her slip and slide over me was hotter than the dirtiest sex I'd had before and after her.

I'd never been closer to heaven than I was when any part of Parker was wrapped around a part of my body.

My fingers.

My tongue.

My cock.

Her mouth.

Her ass.

Her pussy.

She shredded my control even further as she bobbed over me, sucking, licking… goddamn worshipping my dick. And fuck if she didn't make me feel like a god right in that moment. A fucking unworthy deity. Humbled by the intense praise of his most devoted subject.

No. In this relationship I was not the god. Parker was. My goddess.

My love.

My everything.

Electricity raced and popped down my spine, dissolving into the crackling pool at the base of my balls. I gritted my teeth, fighting the signal that my orgasm was much closer than I wanted. Releasing my flesh, I thrust the other hand in her hair, both cradling her head and firmly holding her steady. Her eyes flickered to mine, and the lust raging through me rocketed from consuming to combustible. Pleasure darkened her gaze so much it appeared black. A spark of impatience flashed in the depths, and in spite of the need digging its claws low in my gut, a corner of my mouth quirked into a tight smile as feral satisfaction curled in my chest.

"Open," I ordered, not waiting for her obedience but rolling my hips up and nudging her lips. I pressed inside, pushing deeper, sinking more than half of my length inside of her mouth and pressing the tip just down her throat for a moment. I pulled back as Parker flattened her tongue, offering me even more access straight to the back of her throat.

A groan tore from me, my control ripping at the seams. "That's it, baby. Let me in." It wasn't a demand, it was a goddamn, guttural plea. Parker rose higher onto her knees, bent lower over me, and grateful, that she offered this to me, I leaned down, and pressed a kiss to her damp forehead. Then, I straightened, as I slowly guided her down my cock.

"Fuck," I snapped as the head bumped the entrance to her throat and slipped a little into that tight-as-fuck channel. I grunted, the only sound I was capable of uttering in that moment. My lungs seized as I withdrew then pressed forward once more, taking another increment of her throat. Feeling it spasm and flutter around my tip.

"Goddamn," I snarled. The last remnants of my control disintegrated, and my dick pistoned in and out of her. Fucking her.

Use me. Use me.

The words spurred me on, making me thrust harder. Her nails pinched my thighs, and I hesitate for a moment, but no sound of protest emanates from her lips. No, she continued to suck at me like she couldn't get enough, her entire world narrowed down to my flesh in her mouth, and mine on her.

Always her.

Lightning snapped through me, and I hurtled toward an orgasm that might indeed fucking kill me. But, fucking hell, what a way to go.

My balls tightened and draw up, and if unclenching my teeth were a possibility, I would have warned Parker about coming. About my seed bursting for to pour down her throat. Ask if she was okay with it, since it wasn't something we'd ever done before. But I couldn't, so I didn't. "The little death" nailed me, and I exploded, growling through it like the beast the military has made me out to be. From my brain to the hot, burning soles of my feet inside my boots, I was land-locked by pleasure so keen, so sharp, it bordered on pain. Worse and so much better than the torture I endured in a German terrorist cell.

I came so violently, a part of me recoiled at what I'd become. Some feral animal gripping his female tight as he poured into her over and over. When I was finally, *finally*, spent, I released Parker's head and fell against the back of the couch, harsh breaths exploding from my chest, residual pulses tripping over my skin and down my spine. Parker placed an absurdly gentle kiss on the tip, then lifted her head.

That kiss.

It completely undid me.

Though she'd just sucked my brain through the head of my fucking, aching, "nine-inch monster" — as she used to call it — it was that kiss that caused me to reach down, ball her tank top in my fist, and drag her up my body. She willingly clambered onto my lap, straddling it. Even though I'd just come hard enough to forget my own goddamn name, my dick thumped.

I couldn't blame it. Parker's shorts may have separated us, but the heat of her penetrated the cotton. Tipping my head back, I tunneled my fingers through her hair once more. I couldn't help myself. I wanted to see those strands released and draped over her shoulders and chest, playing hide-and-seek with those beautiful breasts of hers which had grown bigger thanks to being pregnant with our daughters. Stuck to her sweat-dampened skin. I needed to wrap the heavy weight of it around my fist and wrist, drag her head back, expose that slender throat to my teeth as I fucked her from behind.

"Kiss me," I rasped. "Give me what my dick just had."

I'm so starved to feel Parker's mouth on my own, my gut clenched, going concave. Fuck it, honestly? I was ready to beg. Parker lowered her head, putting her lips on me. But not on my mouth. On my chin. My jaw. My temple. She brushed a caress over the scar at the edge of my jaw and my right ear, that I was so sure she hadn't noticed. My heart pounded at the tenderness, the affection that resided in the light touches.

My eyelids received the same gentle, but sensual, treatment and I held my breath—literally held my goddamn breath like some smitten teenager—when those lips hovered above mine. And when that first sweet rub of her mouth to mine came, a shudder rippled through my body, like a fucking earthquake, and as unmanning, as revealing as it was, I remained still, aching for another. She'd never kissed me like that before; and if she had, I don't think I'd ever been broken enough, desperate for her touch, so starved for the refreshing drink of her mouth to recall it. To need it. To absorb it.

It was the kind of kiss that said, I love you in spite of everything. I want all of you.

I forgive you.

With a growl that generated from the swirling and ever-tightening knot in my chest, I jerked her head down. Desperate to banish the guilt that threatened to eat me from the inside out, to expel the anger at her that taunted me with the possibility of ruining our reunion, I opened my mouth under hers and drove my tongue between her lips.

Hard.

My growl rumbled into a groan at my first hit of her sweet, sultry taste. Just as always it was addictive, and though I was licking the roof of her mouth and curling my tongue around hers at that very moment, I was already hurting for the next time, the next high. She met me, thrust for thrust, suck for suck, lap for lap, and nip for nip — giving as good as I was dishing out. And all with a sexy little whimper that I swallowed and took as my reward for returning to her. For accepting the girls without a blink.

For still loving and wanting her.

Fingers tangled in my hair, her lips parted wider, and she tilted her head to the side, deepening this mouth-fucking innocuously labeled a "kiss". Because we were definitely fucking. Screwing. Getting wet, nasty, wild. Tongues glided, coiled, and danced. Teeth clacked. Lips slid and mated. And below… Below, Parker rubbed that hot, no-doubt soaked sex over my thickening cock.

Dropping both hands to her ass, I cupped the firm, rounded flesh and urged her on, helping her find a rhythm that had me gritting my teeth and rolling my hips to meet every downward stroke. I didn't give a damn that the cotton was chafing my dick. The ball-tightening pleasure rendered that small detail incidental.

"Touch me," she whispered against my mouth on the tail end of a moan. "Please."

I couldn't resist her request or the ache throbbing in it. Quickly pushing down her shorts, I slipped one hand inside the thin material and glided it over her silken flesh. No way in hell could I resist not squeezing her pretty ass before sliding down until my fingertips teased the entrance to her sex. I circled the hole, eliciting a gasp from the woman twisting and bucking on my thighs. That soft, hungry sound quivered between us, and it goaded me on. I dipped my other hand between the front of her shorts and lower belly, not stopping until I brushed her sweet little clit. She jerked as if electrocuted, her back arching so hard she resembled a tightly drawn bow.

Her fingernails dented my shoulders through my T-shirt, and I grunted at the slight sting. Savored it. Hoped when I looked in the mirror tomorrow, there were marks decorating my skin.

Not enough. Not enough.

The words chanted through my head, gaining volume and speed until it was an erotic drumbeat against my skull. I surrendered to that call without putting up any fight. I removed my hands from her, and her disappointed, frustrated whimper ended on a shocked note as I wrenched her from my lap and swiftly switch positions with her. Settling her in the corner of the couch, I knelt on the floor and yanked her shorts and panties down and off. She released a strangled cry and tried to close her legs, tried to hide her hairy, naked sex from me. Tried. Because I didn't allow it.

I palmed the insides of her thighs, pushed them apart, widened them so I had an unhindered, front-seat view to the prettiest, lushest, most perfect pussy I'd ever seen. Maybe because the dark curls and petal soft, swollen folds were drenched with evidence of the desire I'd stirred in her. Maybe because her clit was engorged and pulsing, peeking out from between her lips. Maybe because it was Parker. But the sight of her bare mound waiting for me, wet and clenching was the most beautiful piece of art I'd ever seen in my life.

Bending my head, I trailed my lips up her leg, nuzzled the crease where the limb and torso connected. Inhaling, I dragged her heady, delicious scent into my lungs. Growling, I dove in and lost myself. Long licks up her slit. Thirsty pulls at the swollen nub. Hard, insistent sucks at the folds several shades darker than her skin. Plunging thrusts of my tongue in her sex.

Fucking hell. How did she taste different and yet so much better than I remembered?

Tilting her hips up and back, I angled my head and buried my tongue inside her.

So good. So goddamn, fucking good.

I couldn't get enough. I was a fucking animal. A ravenous, insatiable animal who couldn't help but eat, feed, devour on my favorite meal of all time.

Parker.

Parker's juices.

Parker's quim.

Parker's slit.

Parker's clit.

I was a fucking addict and I didn't ever want to be cured.

Her nails scraped over my scalp, scored my shoulders. She undulated and writhed beneath my mouth — trying to get closer or escape me, shit, I didn't know. But when her soft, choking screams fill my ears, and she started to grind her flesh against my mouth, I got closer.

"Logan, oh God, please. Please. Harder. More," she begged in a hoarse, almost broken voice. *Definitely getting closer*.

Lifting my head, I pinned her in place with a glare and a harsh question. One I desperately needed an answer to.

"Whose is this?" I asked.

She swallowed but didn't answer.

I pushed harder, leaning down and licking her lips.

"Whose. Is. This?"

"Y-yours," she cried out, covering her mouth with her hands.

Taking what belonged to me, I drove two fingers deep inside of her. And damn near howled at the immediate vise-grip of her slick, smooth, muscular walls. My cock, fully recovered and stiff against my lower stomach, pounded in jealousy. It wanted in that snug, hot embrace. Yeah, couldn't blame the beast. Lowering my head, I trailed the tip of my tongue along the path at the back of her pussy, following the smooth patch to the puckered hole hidden between her ass. She stiffened, displaying the first signs of uncertainty since I put my mouth on her. Of course, that didn't stop me from tracing the back entrance, from dipping just inside the tight pucker of her ass.

"Logan," she objected, pushing at my head, and I lifted my mouth as she wished, but replaced it with my finger. Not entering but tapping it, delicately circling it. Teasing her with the knowledge that I wanted in that forbidden tight channel no one had breached.

Rearing up, I latched onto her clit, flicked and stabbed the flesh with the stiffened point of my tongue. Abandoning her ass — for now — I shifted my touch back to her sex and drove inside. Finger-fucked her.

Goddamn. I could do that all night. Screw that. Forever. Just as I always planned.

I would simply set up camp and establish a frontier town right there between my woman's thick thighs. But her steady stream of cries, which she tried to muffle with her hands and a pillow from the couch, her desperate clutching of my head and frantic thrusts of her hips telegraphed she was close and wasn't going to last. And no matter what I wanted; Parker came first.

She always did.

Besides, I longed to feel that bruising, orgasmic grip again. It had been years and I couldn't wait any longer. Wanted to hear that keening wail, even if she had to cover it because our daughters slept somewhere in the house. I was hungry to once again witness the flush and swell of her folds while in the middle of her release.

I captured her clit between my lips, grazed it with my teeth. Lightly bit it. Just hard enough to inflict the edge of pain while my fingertips pressed against and massaged that place high up in her core that would set her off like a bomb. It did. She detonated. And it was beautiful.

She was beautiful.

I didn't let up on her, ensuring she received every last shudder and shake. Only then did I reluctantly straighten, knowing if I surrendered to the urge to continue licking and sucking it might have been too much for her sensitive flesh. The thought of her discomfort is the one thing that could curb the lust ripping at me. Standing, I stared down at her. Half-naked, legs sprawled wide, chest rising and falling on deep, loud breaths… Hair tousled and tangled around her shoulders, neck, and face… Eyes closed as she drifted off to sleep on the couch, lashes a dark fringe…

For years, I'd imagined that very moment. How she'd looked after having my face between her legs again. How I'd feel, watching her, her taste in my mouth, on my tongue. Nothing my mind conjured had compared with reality. The fantasies and daydreams I'd engaged in over the years without her paled in comparison to having the real thing there in front of me.

I didn't care if I had to weaken Parker's defenses with my lips, tongue, fingers, and cock in order to get her to let me back in her and the girls' lives. I would do whatever I had to in order to make sure my family was right by my side when I left Arlington. The tiny hairs on the back of my neck let me know that trouble was coming, and I'd be damned if I left them here while I went to handle it.

Parker was just going to have to get used to passing out on the couch after I ate her to orgasm night after night, until she finally agreed to be mine again.

And then she'd have to get used to it because she belonged to me and that pussy was mine.

CHAPTER SEVEN

LOGAN, PARKER & THE LITTLE GERMAN

Parker Leon
2019

I woke up at four o'clock the next morning as I always did, to check on the girls and to make a cup of coffee. I felt a little bad that I'd all but forgotten my duties as a mother the night before in my quest to suck off Logan and to feel his facial hair rubbing against the inside of my thighs. While it was definitely a step in the right direction for our "re-relationship" it still chafed at me that I hadn't gone to check on the girls once the entire night. Though they hadn't made a peep once. Not even with all the screaming Logan had me doing once we'd gone into my bedroom.

My face grew hot as I remembered all of the wicked things he'd done to my body before and after we'd fallen asleep.

Mmm. It was still as good as it always was. Better, honestly.

Lifting his arm from around my waist I tried to wiggle out from beneath his tight grasp. The entire night Logan had held me tightly in his arms, preventing me from laying too far away from him. As if he were refusing to let anything come between us again. I had never felt as safe as I had while laying with him, and if I didn't love my children as much as I did, there was nothing that would have made me get out of bed and away from my sexy man.

My sexy man?

Oh, who was I kidding? Logan was mine and I was his. There was no sense in even fighting it any longer.

"Where you going?" Logan's voice was rough and sleep-filled behind me, and I turned with a soft smile pulling my lips up. Leaning down I placed a gentle, loving kiss on his mouth.

"I'm just going to go and check on the girls. Go back to sleep," I told him.

Logan shook his head, his blond hair sliding against the pale pink fabric of my pillowcases. "Nope. I told you, you're mine. We're together now. And those are my daughters as well." He sat up and pulled me close to him, sinking his fingers into my sleep-tousled hair.

Damn. Forgot to put on my silk bonnet last night.

He kissed me possessively for a long minute. So long in fact, that when he lifted his head after, I felt slightly dazed and almost forgot what I'd intended to get up to do. As a matter of fact, going back to bed sounded like a great idea.

Logan wagged his finger at me as if he knew my thoughts and shook his head with a self-satisfied smirk on his face. "No ma'am. We have to go and take care of our children, then you and I can come back and play President and Intern," he waggled his eyebrows at me, causing me to giggle, something I hadn't done in years.

"Who's the intern?" I asked as I copied his movements and got out of bed to get dressed in comfortable clothing.

"I'll play you for it. We'll do a bit of 69 action and whomever comes first has to be the intern," Logan suggested.

I glanced up from tying my shoes and smiled at him. Once I was finished, I rose and walked over to stand in front of him. Wrapping my arms around him, I lifted up on my tiptoes so I could kiss him softly.

"What was that for?" Logan asked with a gentle smile.

I shrugged. "I love that you can be both dirty and considerate at the same time."

Logan nodded as if he understood exactly what I was still unable to say. "I love you too."

My breath caught in my throat, and when Logan held out his massive hand, I took it without another thought.

We walked to the bedroom Noelle and Holly shared, looking down into their beautiful faces, before we turned and hand-in-hand we walked into my living room, calling out for *Khal Drogo*©, the name Logan had given to his new puppy. I started to grow worried when the little fluffball didn't appear until I heard his paws scratching at the door… to the front door.

Frowning, I walked over to open the door. *Khal Drogo* was trembling, and without thinking I dropped down to my knees, wrapping my arms around him, just I would do one of my girls. I was so glad I'd gotten the space heaters for my porch as Rachel had suggested, or who knew what I would have found when I opened the door. It had been less than 30 degrees outside the night before.

How would we have explained that to the girls?

"Khal? How'd you wind up outside?" Logan asked the dog, handing me a blanket. "You didn't let him out before we went to bed last night, did you?" he questioned me, not necessarily looking at me suspiciously, but confusion and amazement definitely darkening his gaze.

"No, of course not," I said. "Besides, when would I have had time? You barely let me out of your arms long enough to go to the bathroom."

Logan smirked, before his face cleared and he studied the area outside of my front door with a look of intent and dangerous contemplation.

Deciding I would leave him to his thoughts, I lifted the trembling dog in my arms, and walked him over the fireplace, laying him back down in the bright pink dog bed the girls had *insisted* he needed. I was just about to turn away when I noticed a framed picture on my mantle that didn't belong.

Lifting it I frowned at the image. It was of Logan and the girls. From the night of the fire, and there was her climbing out of her car. Who'd taken the picture? And why the fuck would they think I would want a souvenir of that night?

My hand trembled the moment I saw the small piece of paper protruding from the back. I was distantly aware of Logan walking up behind me, the back of my body became overly sensitive as his heat began to meld with the warmth already spreading through my body, but I had to ignore him for the moment. There were more important things to focus on.

Instead, I opened the back of the frame and lifted out the small sheet of paper, noting the photo paper the picture of her, Logan, and the girls had been printed on. It looked… familiar. It almost looked as if it had come from the copy machine at her school.

That was something I'd have to worry about later. At that moment my attention had to be on the letter left for me.

In my home. When I was sleeping. With my daughters down the hall. By someone I didn't know obviously because they'd left Khal Drogo out on the porch and that was something no one who truly knew me would do.

Good evening Principal Parker (or is it morning when you're reading this, I wonder? You and the Marine seemed to be quite busy when I came by to visit):

My associates and I have a proposition for you. And it's one I do believe you'll want to think about and carefully consider before making a decision on.

You see, we know your Marine. The man who is the father of your children. We made his acquaintance in Germany. We were having such a lovely time with him when some friends of his allowed him to leave... all without saying goodbye.

But before he left, your little soldier-boy took something that didn't belong to him. Something we desperately need back. Something that if it's not returned would make things very uncomfortable for us. We would love your... assistance in getting it back.

Before you say no, Miss Leon, I want you to think about how easily I entered your home and left your daughters' precious dog outside. No one who would have reported me, noticed, and those who did see me won't say a word. Tonight, it was simply an introduction, but the next time we meet it will be for me to receive your answer.

You will determine if it's the last "parent-teacher meeting" you ever have.

I will have your receptionist inform you of the time and place.

Sincerely,

Wolfgang

P.S. If you don't want anything to happen to your children, I suggest you get rid of the Marine. For good. Before something... permanent happens to them.

Fear pulsed through me and I covered my mouth. Someone was after Logan. Someone who was bold enough, and dangerous enough to enter my home and leave a letter threatening my daughters' life without a blink. I loved Logan, but nothing was more important to me than Noelle and Holly.

I turned to Logan to break things off with him, for the safety of our daughters. To get information. To obtain whatever item it was that he'd stolen...

To break both of our hearts all over again. However, Logan was already shaking his head.

"Don't you even fucking think about it, Parker. I'm not a coward and neither are you. I will protect you and our daughters. I have people in my life who will do the same. And I don't care who I have to fight, who I have to kill… I've waited years to have you again, Park. I have kids now. I have a goddamn family. There's no way in hell I'm letting any of you go."

I stared into his eyes, trying to find a crack of vulnerability, hoping I could get him to relent and give in, but I saw the determination in his gaze. He was serious. And by the clenching of his jaw, I knew that our Christmas plans had changed, it wasn't going to simply be full of songs, eggnog, and presents. Instead, I had the distinct feeling that Logan had every intention of

making the streets of Arlington run red
with the blood of the man who dared to
threaten his family.

This was so not the present I was hoping
to receive this year.

CHAPTER EIGHT

LOGAN, PARKER, AND THE BED

Parker Leon
2019

That night, after basically clinging to my girls, and even cuddling with Khal Drogo, a dog I'd never wanted, I finally stepped away from their bedroom door, the dog curled up at the foot of Holly's bed. I knew he'd be in the bed with Noelle in the morning. The dog seemed to be in love with both of my girls and was a fierce protector. I couldn't blame him. I was the same way.

Their father, of course, had us both beat.

Logan had spent the day calling every guy he'd served in the Marines with who was stateside. He'd barely had to say a word before they each had promised to be there. Coming to help. Coming to shield and protect my daughters and me from whatever nightmare Logan had brought back with him from Iraq.

I should have been furious. I should have put my foot down and demanded that he left my house, but, how could I? Logan was quite literally the man of my dreams. The man I'd thought I could never have again. The only man my heart leapt for.

God, he looked amazing, I thought to myself as I watched him sitting at the kitchen table, pouring over documents and maps with a couple of his friends. I had no idea of what they were doing or where the maps and things led them… even why they needed to be doing it, I just knew Logan looked hot as hell doing it.

"L-Logan," I stammered breathlessly. *Damn it, get it together, Parker.*

Logan looked up, his mouth opened to say something, but whatever he saw on my face had his lips turning up into a sexy smirk.

"You need something baby?" he asked me.

I nodded and held out my hand.

"I need you," I said simply, refusing to go into more detail.

Without a word to his friends, a group of men who'd gone impossibly quiet and still, Logan rose, took my hand, then swung me up into his arms before heading back to my bedroom, closing the door firmly behind us. He pressed me against the cool wood, and I shivered.

I opened my mouth to remind him about the girls, about the danger, but he placed a finger against my lips.

"My boys are here. There's about five of them surrounding the house. Bunked down in tents, or in different areas of the house, not to mention the two we just left in the kitchen. You and the girls are safe." He lowered his head and pressed a kiss against the base of my neck.

And when relief flooded my veins, so did pleasure and passion for the man in front of me who was doing everything in his power to make sure his family was okay. It caused my slit to release moisture into the seat of my underwear and I pressed myself as close to him as I could, tugging his head down to mine for the hottest kiss I could deliver.

The time for talking was over. I needed Logan inside of me.

Now.

🍬 🍬 🍬 🍬

Logan Steele
2019

I wasn't sure what had come over
Parker, but I wasn't about to complain.
When we both needed to breathe, I lifted
my head and stared down at her with what
I can only say was a healthy mixture of awe,
wonder, lust, and love. My woman was the
epitome of Black Girl Magic™. How the hell
had I survived a minute, much less years
without her? The Marines may have honed
and strengthened my body, it may have
helped to make me a better, more
financially stable man, but it hadn't made
me a smarter one.

"Have I told you lately, just how much you mean to me?" I asked her as I stepped even closer to her, eliminating any space between us, whatsoever.

Parker tilted her head to the side and gave me a shy smile. "Not in the last fifteen minutes."

I shook my head. "Forgive me. Allow me to rectify that." I picked her up abruptly, chuckling when she gasped. Turning I walked over to the sliding glass door that led out to the balcony that I'd only discovered that morning and pressed her against it.

Rocking my hips upwards slightly, I let her feel the evidence of my desire for her. I leaned down and licked, sucked, bit, and kissed on the base of her neck, growling as she gasped my name in my ear. My entire body shook with the need to sink into her. With the yearning, the unrelenting urge, to plow into her over and over again until our bodies melted into one another, becoming one being. One entity. One heart and soul.

Parker was my air. She always had been. And as I breathed in the scent of her arousal, as it filled my nose and flooded my lungs, I realized why I'd felt as if I were dying for the past four years.

Because I inhaled for the first time in a long time. And damn. It was good.

Her dark espresso eyes darkened, and dropped to my mouth, my chest, to my thighs where my cock was doing a damn good impression of a steel bar.

"Fuck me Logan," she breathed.

"Lift up your skirt," I ordered, so glad she'd changed into her professional attire, even if I'd been annoyed she'd had to leave for a couple of hours earlier that day for work. That skirt gave me access to all the important bits I needed at that moment. Yearning and hunger sank their claws into my gut. It had been about fifteen minutes since the house settled down, and I couldn't be sure that the girls or even my guys were fully asleep, I knew Kynan and Luca weren't. No doubt the two of them were still in the kitchen going over our strategy for the next few days, they could hear everything in this bedroom, the walls were just that thin, but this *need* I had for Parker couldn't wait. I ached for something to take the edge off, even if I had to get her off then wait another hour to have the entire meal of her body. I was desperate for this appetizer.

The swift catch of her breath reached my ears, and my grip on the balcony door's steel bar threatened to snap the handle into pieces while I waited to see whether she would obey me or not. As I watched, Parker slowly inched her skirt up. The breath in my lungs deepened as the hem raised higher and higher and higher until it was bunched around her upper thighs. But it still wasn't enough. "Higher, baby," I rasped. "And take off your panties. I don't want anything between me and you."

A moment of hesitation, and then… movement. A lift of her hips from the glass behind her, then her hands skimmed down those thick, dark brown legs. A moment later, more thighs appeared until, *fuck*, her soft pussy with its dark curls. Air rushed in and out of my chest. *Goddamn*, she's beautiful. Even after all these years there was still this… innocence about her, something I found so unbelievably sensual. Lowering a hand from the door, I placed it on left thigh. Stroked my palm over her silken skin. Eased my hand between her legs and slid two fingers into the most beautiful place in all of Heaven and Earth.

Wet heat surrounded my digits, and I groaned at the slick tightness. "Wider," I demanded—begged. "Spread your legs wider for me, Baby. Let me in." This time she didn't pause but parted those thighs for me, giving me more access to her.

I shifted closer a little, pushing harder, deeper. Her cry rings out into the room, filling my ears like the sweetest, fucking lullaby. The sting of her fingernails bit into my arm, but she didn't shove me away. No, she clung to me. Lifted into my thrust.

"Logan, please." She whimpered. "Oh God...please."

Shifting all my attention down, I withdrew my fingers, and my jeans strangle my erection as the physical evidence of her desire glistened on my skin. Starving for another taste of her—because I would never have enough of her in my mouth—I brought them to my mouth, licked and sucked them clean. Her flavor… musky, bold, and sweet. That brief taste only made me hungry for more. I needed to lay her flat, hold her wide open, and drive into her over and over again. Hold her open and eat her until she screamed and came in my mouth, on my cock. She made a sound — a cross between a groan and a sigh — and I looked up to find her eyes on me.

Watching me savor her.

Lust gleamed back at me. I grazed her bottom lip with my damp fingers. Her breath puffed over my damp skin, and I pressed down on her tender flesh, then pushed forward until her tongue wrapped around them…until she was tasting herself and me. It might as well have been my cock she was licking and sucking I shuddered so hard.

I shifted my other hand down from the door to cup and squeeze myself. The fierce ache wrapped itself around my lower back, sizzling in my balls. Sliding my fingers free of her mouth, I lowered my hand back to her pussy and thrust. She keened, her hips bucking, raising into my stroke. One of her small hands clamped onto my forearm and the other, flew out and grabbed the steel bar of the door. Head thrown back, delicate throat arched tight, she ground her pelvis against my hand. Fucking it hard.

There's not telling how long we had until someone in the house made a noise that caused us to retreat into the shower to enjoy each other's bodies, but while we had the chance, I was going to wring every moment of pleasure from her that I could. She was going to come for me. I drove into her, burying my thick digits as far as they could go, as hard as that position would allow. But Parker helped me, dancing for me, rolling her hips and meeting every thrust with her own. I pressed the heel of my palm against her clit and rubbed.

Hard.

With a sharp cry, she exploded. Her flesh rippled, seizing me, milking my fingers of every drop of pleasure she could get. I continued to massage that pulsing bundle of nerves, so close to blowing, myself, it would only take one bruising pump to my throbbing length. Her nails bit into my wrist as she held me close, riding me, her serrated gasps a sexy soundtrack that I wanted to make her sing again. Her touch fell away from me, and she relaxed. I pulled free of her hot, wet clasp, slowly.

Arousal raged in me so hot, so wild, I was one living mass of lust and need. I was glad we made it through the appetizer of our passion without being bothered. But next came the entrée and I was determined to get mine. To bust a nut deep inside of her hot, tight pussy, and only death would stop me.

I tunneled my fingers into the tight bun she'd pulled her hair up into, and jerked the strands free, tugging her towards me, uncaring of the hairpins that collided down to the floor. The kiss I gave her is the exact opposite of the one she'd given me the night before. It was wild, ravenous, and sloppy. There was not gentleness. No softness. It was rough. Hard.

Desperate.

I slanted my head and dove into her, our tongues battled, twisted, tangled, sucked. She gripped my hair, her nails scratched my scalp, the little prickles only shoving the fire burning me alive to nuclear.

"I'm coming inside of you tonight," I growled against her mouth. "Multiple times. I'm going to fuck you hard tonight. Then I'm going to make love to you. If that's not what you want, then say something now, and I'll go sleep out in the living room. But if you let me stay here tonight, I'm not leaving this room in the morning until I've had you in every way I've been fantasizing about for the last few years and I get you pregnant again."

My hand tightened in her hair. Damn it. I didn't mean to let that last part slip. I prayed to God she didn't catch it. Fucking love made you lose your damn mind and control over your mouth. But when Parker simply nodded, I breathed a side of relief. Nothing on her face or in her eyes reflected confusion or even surprise at my words.

Palming her face, I tilted her head back and crashed my mouth to hers. Hunger edged in desperation. As often as my tongue drove between her lips, and as eagerly as she met me, giving me back every stroke, every lick, every moan, it still was not enough. *Goddamn. Will it ever be enough?* Impatient, I cupped the back of her thighs and hoisted her into the air. Her legs immediately locked around my waist, and I shifted my hands to her ass, groaning as her flesh fills them.

My body trembled when she whimpered.

"Look at you," I groaned. "You missed me. Didn't you baby?"

"Yes, Daddy," she moaned.

I fucking shivered like a little boy. It had been way too long since I'd heard Parker call me "Daddy." No one had known that Parker and I engaged in a little

BDSM play when no one else was around. But hearing those words leave her lips, listening as she called me "Daddy," I couldn't resist. I squeezed and molded, spreading her cheeks slightly apart through the thin material of her skirt, before bringing my hand down firmly on her full, thick, round ass. She gasped, jerked her mouth from mine, and stared down at me, arousal and need meshing in her dark eyes.

I could only guess at what she felt. The slight stinging of my smack and the tingling stretch of that tight ring of muscle. I wanted in that tiny hole. Wanted to watch it stretch around my finger, then my cock. Imagining the constriction of that smooth-as-glass passage as I worked her open for me had my chest rising and falling quicker than before. As if I were marching through the desert with my rucksack on my back.

My dick hardened to the point of pain. Seeking to ease some of it, I ground her down on me, rolling her over my length. Her whimper and my grunt mated in the air, melding into one needy sound. *One more.* Just one more of those teasing strokes. I dragged her over me again, using my grip to circle her skirt-covered flesh over me, bumping the head of my erection against her bare slit, and hauling a hiss from my throat. Yeah, her clothes and mine separated us, but fuck if I couldn't feel the heat of her sex teasing me. Taunting me. But I would have her body. Have her.

Forever, my inner voice promised.

"Can… can we turn off the light?" Parker stammered out and I stared down at her in confusion.

"What?" I asked, shaking my head. We'd kept the lights off the night before just because I hadn't thought to turn them on.

But she had me all the way fucked up if she thought I wasn't going to look at every delectable inch of her body in the light as I took her over and over again and made her mine once more.

Parker bit her lip as she looked up at me. "This is ridiculous. I've never had any issues with my body. I mean, it's not like you didn't know I was a curvy woman before you left. I don't know why… I-I… I-It's just that, since the girls…" She trailed off, shaking her head.

I blinked, understanding crashing into me. *The hell?* She couldn't possibly have doubts about whether I still found her attractive, could she?

God, didn't she know that to me, she was perfect? Didn't she know that no one, no woman, could ever compare to her? That she was it for me? No, how could she? I left her, tried to stay away longer, didn't think about how she would feel, and I'd confessed to her late the night before that I'd slept with other women, while she'd been saving herself, subconsciously, for me to return. Of course she would be uncertain if I still found her attractive, especially after giving birth to our daughters.

But damn, couldn't she see that I hadn't been able to conceal my hunger or my dick around her lately?

"You have that backward," I said into the silence. Her gaze jerked from the wall behind me to my face. "None of those women were you, you are the only one I want. The only one I've ever wanted. No one could replace you, and no one will ever be as beautiful to me as you."

Her lips parted, and she stared at me for several long seconds. A softness entered her eyes, and slowly, she lowered her arms as a light entered her gaze and a teasing smile came to her lips.

"Not even Gabrielle Union?" She teased.

She knew Gabrielle Union was my weakness but as I compared my celebrity crush with the woman who stood in front of me who looked just a bit like her — totally a coincidence, that — I knew there was absolutely no competition. There never was when it came down to Parker and other women.

I shook my head. "Not even Gabby Union."

The big grin that came to her face, the final sigh of relief… signals of trust, of vulnerability, they refueled the need inside me. The need to get my hands, mouth, dick on and in her.

"Take off your clothes," I ordered, not bothering to tone down the harshness in the command. By now, she remembered who she'd invited into her bedroom, into her body. I'd never been a gentleman or poet. I was a rough, half-civilized Marine, who came from nothing, scrapped and fought for everything I had in my life, including her, with zero pretty words. Her response was to peel her shirt off over her head, then pull down the zipper at her hip, and push her skirt down her legs, leaving her in only a pale-yellow bra.

Goddamn.

"Go on," I urged, and she obeyed, popping the front clasp of her bra, and soon, that joined the rest of her clothing on the floor.

Fuck, she was gorgeous. A pagan goddess worthy of worship. Her elegant neck sloped down to delicate shoulders and large, firm breasts with their big, dark-brown nipples that filled my hands like they were created for them. With an adorable, round belly that gave testament to the fact that she'd carried my children, that she was a woman with curves, and toned, if thick, thighs and shapely legs, Parker was any man's vision of a sensual, beautiful woman. And then there was the softest pussy between those thighs... The impulse to rush her and fall on her like a predator with its prey rode me hard. I wanted to take her in big, ravenous bites until this hunger for her was satisfied. But another, stronger longing reverberated in me, propelling me forward, shoving me to my knees in front of her. My arms wrapped around her, and I pressed my forehead to the smooth skin between her breasts.

The musk from her recent orgasm intertwined with her natural scent, and if any company could bottle the fragrance, they would make a killing at any perfume counter. It was sweet and alluring, a magical potion that in turn drove a man wild and made him want to genuflect in awe and reverence. And that was what I was to her, though she had no idea.

A devotee.

A worshipper.

Her hands tunneled through my hair and cradled my head. And that quick, lust amped up to compete with veneration. My hold on her tightened, and I turn my head, capturing a nipple between my lips. A shudder shook her, a moan drifting above my head. Her nails scratched my scalp, and I growled against her flesh, coiling my tongue around the stiff peak, and sucked. She released one of those sexy whimpers that have become my sexual currency, and I tugged on the tip, grazing it lightly with my teeth before drawing on it again.

"Logan," she whined, bending over me, pressing her cheek to the top of my head. "Oh God, please. I need…"

I already knew what she needed. And switching to the other breast and licking the pebbled point, I eased a finger between her legs. Her hips bucked against my hand, a cry tearing from her as I traced a circle around her clit. The rich scent of her arousal was thicker, and my mouth watered for a taste. Giving her nipple one last suck, I trailed my lips down her stomach, pausing to dip inside her navel, then continuing down, nuzzling the thatch of damp curls, before replacing my finger with my tongue. Her choked scream was a symphony to my ears. Then I didn't hear anything but the dull roar in my ears as I teased and lapped at that nerve-filled bundle of flesh.

I groaned into her sex, drowning in her flavor, the silken texture of her. I couldn't help myself; I feasted on her. Suckled her, stroked through her folds, nipped the swollen lips sticky with the evidence of her arousal, lowered my head to plunge my tongue inside her. I was a starving man who'd pulled up to a table heavy with every temptation he'd ever craved. But I was still hungry. I slid a finger inside her, coating it in her wetness. I couldn't resist a couple of heavy thrusts, my knuckles bumped against her folds. With a low cry, she widened her legs, giving my hand more room. But as much as I loved being inside her, I wanted something else, *needed* something else.

Following the path that connected her sex to her ass, I dipped between her crease and lightly trace the tiny entrance there. She stiffened, her hands freezing on my head. But I didn't stop caressing her, letting her become accustomed to my touch on the place where I knew no man had ever been.

"Logan?" she whispered, a quiver in her voice.

My answer was to rake my teeth over that pulsing nub and suck even as I drenched my finger in her wet heat again and returned to her ass. This time, I pressed, not entering but firmly resting my fingertip there. Her hips rolled against my mouth, a steady stream of mixed whimpers and muted screams escaping her. I refused let up, tormenting her clit with my tongue, so when I did slip my finger into the constricted ring of muscle, she only tensed up a little, and her cry of pleasure only contained a hint of pain.

I held still, didn't slip any farther into the channel, but I didn't let up on her pussy. I tongued it hard, granting her no mercy. And as she emitted a long, rumbling moan that had me throbbing, I pushed deeper into her.

She exploded.

She quaked against my face, riding it, her legs trembling, her torso curling over my shoulder. Between the clench of her ass, the pulsing of her clit, and her gasping sobs, I could have come right there, kneeling on her bedroom floor, my face buried in the closest to heaven I'd likely ever get near. As her quaking ebbed into shivers, I finally lifted my mouth from her, fighting the urge to dive back in, to make her come again.

And again.

Maybe she sensed the struggle within me, because she weakly pushed at my head. I gave in, but only because if I didn't get inside her right that minute, I was extremely afraid my dick might just grow sentient and rise up to kill me. I straightened, with Parker over my shoulder in a fireman's carry. Crossing the short distance to the bed, I laid her on it, my cock cursing even that amount of time.

Next time we'll fuck her against the balcony door. I promised the dark red member that spurt out another stream of precum.

Her lashes fluttered closed, her chest still rising and falling quickly, but her body was loose, relaxed. Grabbing a fistful of my T-shirt, I jerked it over my head and dropped it to the floor. My jeans and boxer briefs quickly joined it and I tossed them on the bottom of the mattress. As I approached the bed, Parker's eyes opened and met mine. A heat shimmered there, one that reflected the flames licking at me from the inside out. Wrapping my fingers around my length, I squeezed it, both easing and heightening the ache. My balls drew up, but I willed the looming orgasm back from the crumbling edge. I circled her slender ankle, then stroked my palm up the length of her leg until my fingertips grazed the flesh I'd just devoured.

Her breath caught, her back arching, those beautiful breasts rising toward the ceiling. I tightened my grip on my cock, the flash of pain momentarily clearing my head, shoving the lust back just enough that it kept me from climbing on top of her, burying myself in her, and putting us both out of this beautiful misery quickly, like a motherfucking animal. I lifted a knee to the mattress, leaned over her, splayed my fingers over her stomach and glided that hand up her soft stomach, between her breasts, and around her throat. She stared at me, that same fire that was always in her chocolate gaze whenever I choked her slightly growing hotter and darker.

And when I exerted the slightest pressure, just the slightest, the flames grew deeper. She liked it—she always had—the control, the hint of roughness, the dirtiness I displayed when we were in bed together like that. Suddenly, my fist around my cock wasn't enough to hold back the conflagration of lust threatening to consume me. I needed to be inside her, that slick, tight, wet, almost bruising embrace locked around me.

"Roll over, baby," I rasped, and with a grasp of her hip, helping her flip. She went up to her hands and knees without further prompting, that big, perfect ass of hers in the air, the swollen, glistening folds visible and a lure to dive back in and lose myself once more surged within me. I growled as I twist my fist in her hair, savoring the silken caress of her relaxed hair.

"Logan." Parker glanced over her shoulder. "Please. Fuck me."

The request was gasoline poured over a ten-alarm fire. Scattering kisses down her spine, I circled the base of my cock, aligned it with the entrance to her pussy…and sank inside.

Slowly.

Steadily.

Until I was surrounded by her. Branded by her. Once more owned by her.

I clenched my jaw, preventing myself from weeping like a little bitch at how amazing my woman felt surrounding me, as I pulled free of her body, dragging through her muscular walls that clutched at me, as if trying to prevent me from leaving her. When only the head remained just inside her, I pushed back in, groaning. Pleasure struck at the base of my skull, sizzling down my spine, and culminated like an electrical storm in my balls.

One stroke.

One goddamn stroke, and I was so mother fucking ready to blow, I was shaking with the need to release. It was like soaking the lower half of my body in a hot tub while simultaneously being dunked headfirst in the coolest, most welcoming pool. Her back arched, head thrown back, all that hair stuck to her damp skin. I should have closed my eyes, because looking at her would have had me filling her tight pussy with the next thrust.

But I couldn't. Not when I'm hoarding every second of this for when I have to leave again. For those moments when I had to return to duty, and she was back here in the States. When I was alone, with only my hand and memories for company.

Abandoning her hair, I clasped her hips, and plunged deep. Over and over, I drove into her, savoring each plunge, each suck of her flesh releasing and welcoming me, each cry that broke on her lips, each shudder that coursed through her. I shifted my hands lower, cupped her ass…spread the cheeks, exposing the tiny hole I teased earlier.

Just like before, it lures me, and I want inside of it so fucking bad. Dipping a finger to where we're connected, I slid it through her soaked folds, and drew the drenched tip around the entrance. Unlike last time, I don't wait, but slipped it inside. Again, she stilled, tensed, pausing mid-stroke so only half of my shaft was buried inside her. Her harsh, loud pants echoed in the room, and I continued to press forward, inching more and more of my finger in her ass.

"Relax, baby," I murmured, damn near choking on the groan as I slowly filled the narrow channel. It was so small, so tight, I would have had to work to stretch it so she could take me. My hips jerked at the thought, shoving more of myself inside her. She keened, low and deep, and electrical charges tripped through me, marching up and down my spine, lighting me up. "Relax and push back against my finger. You can take me, just like before."

Her head dropped forward, her hair a dark curtain over her shoulders and hanging around her face. She did as I instructed, shifting backward, taking my cock and my finger. Watching it, I was like a horse with blinders, unable to look away, completely focused on the sight of me sinking into both entrances.

Fucking hell, how did I go so long without this. Without her?

I flexed my hips, thrusting into her, and pushed the rest of my finger deep into her. Her scream rebounded off the walls, and the piercing sound shattered my control. I fucked both parts of her again and again, riding both her pussy and ass hard. And she took it, fucking craved it, if the way she backed into me, harder, faster, her sobs damn near incoherent, were any indication.

I shifted my free hand from her hip, swept it down her lower belly and between her legs, seeking out and locating her clit. One stroke, two, over the bundle at the top of her sex, and her slick muscles clamped down on me.

"Fuck!" I growled just as she came, shaking, crying, her walls rippling around me, milking me. I dropped down over her, pressing my chest to her spine, my palms bracketing her head. My hips snapped back and forth, pounding into her, taking, claiming…

My orgasm barreled through me, snatching the air from my lungs, goddamn nearly blinding me. It was pleasure, agony, ecstasy. An abyss that I catapulted myself into like an Olympic diving champion… or a suicide jumper. And as I sank to the mattress, my arms wrapped around this woman who I craved and loved more now than I had four years previous, fuck if I can tell which one I'd become. I just knew one thing.

I would die before I let anyone take this from me.

CHAPTER NINE

THE BAR FIGHT

Logan Steele
2019

I couldn't believe I'd let Kynan and the rest of the guys talk me into going to the bar. Granted, Parker had agreed to come with us, letting Noelle and Holly go and spend the night with her friend Rachel's kids and her NFL husband, but still…

I'd much rather be at home filling Parker's tight hole with my cum again.

When the unattached, single guys began to laugh and tease those of us in the group who were in committed relationship, I simply clutched Parker tighter to me. My heart swelled when she sighed and sank into my embrace. This right here was heaven.

"I'll be right back," Parker breathed, pressing her lips against the curve of my jaw. I clenched my teeth as I swallowed back my growl. Where the fuck did she think she was going? She was wearing a thin, green sweater dress, that stopped mid-thigh. I wanted her by my side, where no fucking asshole could get any ideas.

When she giggled, I looked down, quirking my eyebrow.

"You look like you're about to attack every man in this bar." She rolled her eyes. "I'm just going over to the bar," she told me, placing a light kiss on my lips.

I nodded and released her; my gaze trained on her plump ass as she went.

"Fucking hell, Loge. I thought I was sprung, but your woman got your nose *wide* open," Duane Hall, one of my friends who'd served with me, said with a chuckle.

I looked over at him and gave him an assessing stare. "Aye, don't be checking out my woman though," I warned him.

Duane shrugged. "I mean, I just feel bad for my sista, right? I mean… she's only had white boy dick. Maybe I should show her what she's been missing." He laughed and though I knew he was just joking; I had the insane urge to pummel one of my closest friends into the floor of the bar.

Before I could decide on what I was going to do, Kynan caught my attention.

"Hey, Loge. Who the fuck is that pushing up on your woman?"

I turned and saw a tall, blond man, wearing, of all things a Confederate shirt, one arm on the bar as he talked to Parker. My woman. But when he reached out to stroke a finger along her arm, my vision went red. I hadn't realized that I'd let out a loud roar and jumped across the table, grabbing him and snatching him away from Parker until I felt the flesh of his neck in between my fingers and heard his gasps filling my ears sounding like a goddamn R&B love song, it was so sweet.

I tightened my fist around the other man's throat, leaning closer to his red face, with tears streaming down his face as he gasped for breath.

"Back. Off. She. Is. Mine," I snarled, before tossing him across the room.

Seconds later, a fight broke out.

And thirty minutes after that, the cops showed up.

🍭 🍭 🍭 🍭

Parker Leon
2019

I dare any woman out there who is attracted to men sexually to say that they weren't a little turned on when their man fought for them. When they got a little jealous. When they were willing to risk life and limb in order to make sure that no one tried to take you away from them. Oh, I'm not talking *Investigation Discover* ™, husband killing his wife or her lover, in order to make sure no one tried to take her away from him.

I'm talking getting all up in a mother fucker's face and letting him and every other asshole in the area know that you belonged to him. That he was putting it on you on the regular. That he was the one who made your legs weak. Made your mouth water. That your pussy only got wet and came for him.

What? It's only me. Whatever heifers.

Anyway, I was turned on like a fucking horny cow, just mooing all over the damn place when Logan roared like a lion and attacked the asshole who thought he had the freedom to put his hands on me. And when he lifted that scumbag up into the air like he weighed nothing?

Okay bitches, yes, my fucking panties were soaked.

Even when he tossed him like yesterday's trash, I was panting like a bitch in heat.

But when the fight broke out among almost every guy in the bar?

Well, let's just say this kitty went from being drenched to being dry as the Sahara in a flash.

Then when the police showed up? I was trying everything I could to drag Logan out of the back of the bar with me.

The worse part was when the police came directly over to Logan and asked him questions. When one of them pulled out a pair of handcuffs I began trying to think of how I was going to explain to our daughters why daddy's face was on the television as having been arrested in a bar brawl the night before.

But before I could, Logan was shaking hands with the police officers and thanking them for their prompt arrival and their service.

What. The. Fuck?

I wanted to ask but I couldn't. Logan grabbed my elbow and gathering his friends he ushered us all out of the bar. I kept opening my mouth over and over again to ask questions, but I could never find the right words.

All I knew was that the next day was Christmas Eve, and I had to wrap presents and get them under the tree before my girls found them. Maybe for Christmas Santa would deliver a solution to my problems with Logan, because between him just *showing* back up in my life, the German who was looking for him, and my own feelings for him returning with a fierceness that even surprised me, I was going to need a miracle that only that jolly, white-haired, fat man could bring.

CHAPTER TEN

CHRISTMAS EVE CONFESSIONS & PROMISES

Parker Leon
2019
Christmas Eve

I was so angry I just knew that every step I took, I left behind ash from my flaming footsteps.

After getting in a fight at the bar the previous night, and almost being arrested, a naïve person would have expected Logan to be contrite. To be humble. To take a step back to reevaluate his life. But noooo… not the father of my children. Not the man who said he wanted another chance with me.

Not the man who said he wanted to love me forever.

Instead, I'd gotten up that morning and found Logan outside in my backyard with his friend, Kynan, the two of them snarling, hissing, and spewing profanities like they were fucking animals as they replayed the events of the night before. They were talking as if they had every intention of finding the guys they'd fought and get into another brawl with them.

On fucking Christmas Eve.

And believe me, I know the irony about me complaining about their profanity only to call them "fucking animals", but there's a *big* difference. I said mine internally. I wanted to stick out my tongue at my conscience for trying to make me feel guilty. I was not the one who should be feeling bad right then. No. I was the innocent party. Right there along with the girls. Holly and Noelle who still foolishly believed that their father hung the stars, moon, and sun, just for them. I'd been just as… awed by the changes Logan had gone through since being in the military.

Which was why the disappointment I felt finding out he was still exactly the same hurt so much.

I slammed around the pots and pans in the kitchen, trying to figure out what meal I could make that would be the most gratifying to my current murderous mood. Maybe *crushed* steak? Or *pulverized* meatloaf?

Or *bloody chicken*?

Just as I was about to slam another pot on top of the stove the opening strains of Boyz II Men's "On Bended Knee" © began to play.

I turned around the moment I heard Logan's smooth baritone voice singing.

"Darling, I… I can't explain… where did we lose our way?"

Fuck. I'd always loved his voice.

"If you come back to me… I'll guarantee… I'll never let you go."

I wanted to be so angry with him, but he stood in the middle of my living room, wearing a pair of silk pajama bottoms, with the silk pajama top unbuttoned, and a fan blowing the shirt. Just as if he were in a R&B music video. I would have laughed, if he weren't being so earnest in his apology and begging.

I loved a man who could beg like an R&B singer.

"Oh God give me a reason... I'm down on bended knees."

Logan got down on a knee and liquid rolled down my neck. I reached up to wipe it away, glancing up at the ceiling to see what was leaking. Finding nothing, I touched my cheek. I found more wetness and then it dawned on me.

I was crying.

Logan had me so in my feelings I was crying over him singing along to an old R&B classic.

"So many nights when I dreamed of you... holding my pillow tight..."

At that, Logan pulled out a box from beneath my couch and I frowned. Where had that come from? It wasn't mine. It looked battered. Bruised. Worn. As if it had been moved from one place to another dozens of times.

As if it had endured a war.

When Logan handed me the box, with the top falling off it, the edges frayed, I wanted to shove it back into his hands. I had a feeling that whatever was in that box was going to take away my reasoning for being angry with him.

I needed my anger. Needed to hold onto my rage. My disappointment. My hurt.

Because the minute I let them go, I'd only be left with one emotion when it came to Logan.

Love.

And I just wasn't sure if I were ready to love him again.

Not truly.

"When I opened up my eyes... to face reality... every moment without you... it feels like an eternity..."

I glanced up into Logan's face as he reached out a hand and caressed my cheek. The moment I did, I gasped. My own hurt and pain were reflected in his gaze. My own disappointment. My own anger at where our own choices and decisions had brought us.

I realized then that while Logan had been keeping secrets from me. Secrets that had inadvertently put me and our girls in danger, I had also kept secrets that put us in danger. A part of me had always known that if I told Logan about the twins he would return. He would even give up the military for them—for us—if I'd *really* asked. But I hadn't wanted to ask. On the off chance he said no and chose the military over me and the girls.

It was foolish. It was stupid. And it had hurt so many people.

"I'm begging you, begging you... come back to me..."

Well the answer to that was pretty simple. So, I raised my face and lifted my lips to kiss the man who'd always loved me more than anyone else on Earth. The man who'd risked life and limb to return to me. The man who'd accepted his daughters with no hesitation and loved them so much it made me cry.

I stopped running. I stopped being afraid, and I accepted the love, the passion, and the promises he gave me.

🍬 🍬 🍬 🍬

Logan Steele
2019
Christmas Eve

I was so glad I'd listened to Kynan.
Parker was upset and I had to do something
big to get her to forgive me. While I didn't
think I needed to ask forgiveness for
fighting some asshole fuckwad who
thought to push up on my woman the night
before, according to Kynan and Ava, Parker
wasn't like the other women I'd
encountered in my life. The Marines had
given me amnesia when it came to Parker.
She wasn't necessarily innocent, but she still
tried to see the positive in the world. Even
when it dealt her a bad hand. Which meant
that she was not a woman who would be

impressed with me strolling around the day after a fight figuring out how to get revenge.

No. My woman would want me to be thankful I hadn't been arrested and spend time with her wrapping presents and making Christmas dinner.

They were things I hadn't done in years.

And things I was desperate to do again.

As we kissed, I remembered the year before when I'd known it was time for me to come home. Time for me to temporarily say goodbye to the Marines and go home to reclaim my woman. It was the best decision I'd ever made, and subsequently the hardest thing I'd ever done.

I wouldn't regret it.

🍬 🍬 🍬 🍬

Logan Steele
2018

"Hey Steele! You staying around
with these fucking rag heads again for
another Christmas?" one of the privates
yelled out, no doubt trying to impress his
buddies by trying to rile up someone who
outranked him. I knew what everyone
thought. I was one of the few who didn't
take my furlough and go home to family
and friends. That was because I knew if I
went home and saw Parker. Held her in my
arms again. Kissed her lips. Squeezed that
ass once more?

I wouldn't be returning.

I'd go AWOL with a goddamn smile
on my face.

I loved being in the Marines, but I hated being away from my woman.

"Watch your fucking mouth," I said as I slammed the newbies head down on the table. "Be glad you're in the goddamn Marines," I growled low, next to his ear. "You could have been in the fucking Air Force, cumstain."

And with that I turned to walk away.

I marched away from the chow tent, my angry footsteps kicking up sand as I stomped aimlessly.

"Dude, you need to get laid," Kynan said with a chuckle, where he lay with his head resting against his rucksack, cover laying low over his eyes.

I grunted. "I just slept with that Pakistani woman the other night," I pointed out.

Kynan scoffed and flipped up his middle finger. "No man. You need real pussy. You need to take yourself home and fuck your woman. Let her remind you why you're fucking over here. Why you're serving. Why you're fighting. Let her make you goddamn human again. You've gone beyond animal to being a fucking monster. And growing up with my older brother, father, and uncles, trust me when I say I know monsters."

He stood up and walked towards me until he stopped directly in front of me. He pointed at me.

"You know what you need for Christmas this year? You need some goddamn joy. Some cheer. Some happiness. Some fucking hope." He smirked. "And you need some *snatch-the-soul-out-of-your-chest* pussy." He shook his head. "And you ain't going to get none of that here."

And when Kynan walked away, returning to his previous position of lounging with his head on his sack, I contemplated his words.

And made sure it was the last Christmas I spent alone.

Logan Steele
2019

I stared at Parker, her yes bright with unshed tears as I finished speaking.

"That's why you came home?" she asked me.

I nodded. "I'm not me without you," I told her. "I didn't know who I was becoming. I didn't *like* who I was. It wasn't just because I missed you, Park. I missed *me*. I missed being able to breathe. I missed being able to walk without feeling as if every step caused me immeasurable pain. And I was in pain because I was without you."

I tugged her closer to me. "I made a wish on a star last Christmas. I wished that I would be able to find you. That I would be able to come home to you. And that this time? When I left, I'd have you with me."

I turned my head to glance down the hallway where our daughters were sleeping.

"I'd have you all with me."

Parker sniffled.

"Oh, Logan."

But I didn't let her speak any more. Instead, I took her lips with my own in a deep, hungry kiss.

🍬 🍬 🍬 🍬

Parker Leon
2018

I stared at my daughters where they slept in bed and felt sadness curdling in my belly like rancid milk. I turned away, my hand against my mouth as I struggled not to cry. I walked quickly out of the room and out the back door. I stared up at the night sky and searched for the brightest star.

"I don't know if I actually believe in you, or in Santa more, but whichever one of you is listening. I miss him." I shook my head. "I think I will always miss him. And for as long as I miss him, I will have to deal with this ache in my chest. And it's making it so that I can't breathe."

"I need to be able to breathe. I have kids to raise."

I wiped my tears from my cheeks and blew out a breath.

"So what do I want for Christmas? I want the pain to stop. However you have to do it. Just make it go away."

Logan Steele
2019
Christmas Eve

"Looks like they did," I told her after Parker shared the details of her previous Christmas with me.

She chuckled softly. "I guess they did."

"I love you Park."

"I love you, Lo."

Looking over at the clock, I tugged her naked, still sweaty body closer to me in the bed and placed a gentle kiss on her lips.

"Merry Christmas."

"Merry Christmas."

CHAPTER ELEVEN

CHRISTMAS DAY PROMISES

Parker Leon

2019

Christmas Day

I was used to Noelle and Holly running into the room and screaming with excitement and happiness, Logan and the rest of his friends were not.

So the deep, profanity laced bellows that filled the air as my girls ran from room to room waking everyone up with exclamations that "It's Christmas! Time to wake up!" were forgiven.

Hell, I'd done it the first year they'd done it to me as well.

I laughed and rolled away from Logan, grabbing my robe and pulling it over my naked body. I placed a kiss on his grumpy face and went to the bathroom to handle my morning ablutions. When I'd finished with that, I allowed Noelle and Holly to take my hands and tug me into the living room where the Christmas tree that Logan and Kynan had remembered to buy, stood proudly in the corner of the room.

I blinked in surprise, knowing that there had *not* been that many presents beneath our fake Douglas fir when Logan and I had escaped to the bedroom the night before after making up.

"We… uh… we might have kind of bought some presents for the girls," Kynan confessed scratching at the back of his head sheepishly.

My heart squeezed as I looked around the room at all of the tough, widely muscled, stern — *gorgeous* — Marines who filled my room and had come to protect me and my daughters, all because Logan told them he needed help and felt joy and happiness fill my heart.

I'd felt so lonely and broken-hearted since the death of my parents. Since Logan had left.

Since I realized that even with my friends, it was me and my girls against the world.

But that wasn't the way it was anymore. Logan had returned and he'd brought his own family with him. And I knew without asking that each and every man in that room would go to hell and back to protect Holly, Noelle, and I from every single danger out there in the world.

Just the way a family did.

"It's okay," I said, patting Kynan's shoulder. "You were all just being good uncles." I sniffled and gave them all a bright smile.

"We have unca's?" Holly asked softly where she sat in front of a very large pile of presents that had all been addressed to her.

"That's right my little angel," Logan said with a big grin. "All of these men here are your uncles." He gestured around the room, pausing at me for a moment and tossing me a wink. "And they're always going to be here for you. Just like me and Mommy."

"Pwomise?" Noelle asked.

Logan cleared his throat and nodded. I knew then that no matter my own fears, Logan loved our daughters just as much as I did. I felt a little guilty that they'd been kept apart for so long, but I also believed that things happened when they were supposed to. He may not have been ready before, but Logan Steele the man I loved, my Marine, was ready now.

"I promise," he replied, placing a gentle kiss on both girls' foreheads.

"Come on! Let's open presents!" Luca said with a hearty laugh that seemed oddly out of place coming from his stacked, muscled frame.

"Yay! Pwesents!"

I clutched the cup of hot cocoa one of the Marines had handed me and watched my daughters with adoration, warmth, and love filling me, only to come up short when Logan stood in front of me, appearing almost out of thin air, with a wrapped present in his hand.

A small, tiny, blue velvet box with a red ribbon wrapped around it.

Small enough to hold a ring in it.

Holy. Shit.

🍬 🍬 🍬 🍬

Logan Steele
2019
Christmas Day

I watched Parker's face carefully as she stared at the box before taking it in her hands. I switched out her mug of cocoa for the ring box, handing the mug off to Kynan who stood by my side. Just like always.

As Parker focused on unwrapping the ribbon from the box, I dropped down to one knee.

I raised my eyes up to Parker's the moment she gasped. I took her left hand in both of mine and placed a gentle kiss on the backs of her fingers.

"You made me the man I am today Parker. Once I thought it was the Marines. I thought I would only be a man of substance, of worth, only deserving of you if I went out into the world and made something of myself." I shook my head at my own foolishness. "I thought the only way you could ever *truly* love someone like me was if I had something to offer you, because you'd given me so much."

I shook my head when she opened her mouth to no doubt refute my statement. "But I know now that was my own insecurity putting those thoughts in my head. I was a man of substance, of worth, a man who deserved you, because *you chose me*. Because you said I was. Who am I to argue with a goddess? With the woman who owns my heart? The woman who gave me all of herself…" I turned to look at Holly and Noelle who watched me with curiosity.

"… and so much more? I still don't think I deserve you Parker Leon, but if you will have me, I want to spend the rest of my life trying to be. Please allow me the chance to love you for the rest of my life, and even after I draw my last breath. Will you mar—"

"Yes!" Parker interrupted me.

" —ry me?" I shook my head and laughed. I lifted out the ring and slid it onto the third finger of her left hand. I placed a kiss on it, my eyes sliding closed.

"Thank you."

Parker knelt in front of me and placed a kiss on my lips.

"Thank you for coming home to me and the girls, and for always being my protection."

I gathered her close to me and sighed in relief. "And thank you for being my comfort and joy."

Things weren't settled, not by a long shot. We didn't know who was behind the letter that had been left in Parker's house—not my home as well—though I had my suspicions. And I would have to return to duty at some point.

But for now? Right now I was going to enjoy Christmas with my family.

The way I always would. Forever.

Until I drew my last breath.

Epilogue

Four Christmases Later

🍬 🍬 🍬 🍬

Parker Leon
2023
Christmas Day

I stared at Logan, laughing at his look of complete confusion as he attempted to put together the Christmas dollhouse our three-year-old son had asked for. Logan and I didn't try and force any of our children to conform to gender stereotypes, but I knew in that moment that Logan wished our son, Nick, had simply asked for a racecar.

The way Noelle had.

I rubbed a hand over my bulge which was evidence of my being pregnant with our fourth child. Logan still hadn't left the Marines, though I knew now why he'd stayed in for as long as he had, and why he'd wanted to reenlist.

So that his family had the protection of the US Marine Corps in case anything happened to him.

While the creepy home invader hadn't been back, we'd also moved. I'd said goodbye to Arlington and had allowed Logan and his friend Kynan to move me and the kids to Baltimore where Kynan's brother, Andrew McCarthy, and his wife Kyra, helped to look out for us. And while I wasn't one-hundred percent positive what they were involved, I knew it was something I didn't want to know anything about.

With us under the protection of Andrew and Kyra, Logan had felt a little easier about returning to duty. And resuming his search for the man—or men—who'd threatened his family.

And I wasn't going to begrudge him that.

But I was extremely happy to have him home for Christmas.

Even if he was making a mess and cursing up a blue streak.

"Do we *have* to get him this fucking thing?" Logan cursed.

I shook my head. "You were the one who insisted on building it for him, rather than buying the one that was built already, and you simply had to lower the different floors," I pointed out. I bit my lower lip when Logan growled at me and rose to his feet. I giggled and ran—or rather, waddled — out of the room trying to get away from him.

I appreciated that Logan allowed me to get all the way to our bedroom before he trapped me against the wall, with his hands braced on either side of me.

"You better be careful woman, or I'll put another baby inside of you."

I rolled my eyes. "What, right next to the one that's already in there?"

Logan chuckled. "You're damn right."

"That would be a Christmas miracle."

I shivered as he ran his nose and lips against the side of my neck.

"Well, Merry Christmas to me."

And with that, Logan took my lips in a kiss that wound up with us having to give our son Nick a picture of the dollhouse we were *going* to buy him a few days later that was already pre-assembled the next morning.

A Merry Christmas indeed.

THANKS FOR READING!

🍬 🍬 🍬 🍬

I so hope you enjoy the first book in the For The Love Of The Marines series. I know many of you noticed some familiar faces in this quick Christmas read. That's because while writing 35/F Seeks Alpha (Rachel & Ryan, 1) I realized that all of my books, all of my series were going to intertwine. Or at least the series that have already begun. Which makes it pretty interesting when one of those series is a paranormal. This is a Christmas novella, so it is much shorter than my other works.

This is also the beginning of a series, so while the main couple: Logan and Parker get an HFN, the story as a whole ends on a cliffhanger (Did you figure out who the Little German was?)

Anyway, if you want to sign up for my newsletter and know when I have another book coming out (and to find out what's going on with my author friends), sign up here (I do giveaways all the time):

http://bit.ly/VVeesNewsletter

A VERY ALPHA CHRISTMAS SERIES

Each Story is A Standalone and Books Do Not Have to Be Read in Order

Don't Miss The Other Hot Books in This Series!

1. Her Mistletoe Minotaur-Erin St. Charles
2. X-Mas and Ohs-Francesca Penn
3. Running From Noel-Janae Keyes
4. A Bite of Christmas Cheer-Thea Dane
5. Up to Snow Good-Sydney Aaliyah Michelle
6. His Comfort & Joy- V. Vee
7. Odin's Honor-Reana Malori
8. Her Silent Knight-Siren Allen
9. A Classic Alpha for Christmas-Shani G. Dowdell

About The Author

You Can't Spell Love Without V

V. Vee is just another one of the pennames of USA TODAY and International Bestselling and Award-Winning author V. A. Bailey who also writes under the names: Vicktor Alexander, Veronica Victorian, V. Alex, Leyah, ShaKira, Alexandra Bailey, and Vee Bailey. One of 9 different pennames used by the author, V. Vee is the one dedicated to bringing to life the love between men and women in interracial, multicultural, and non-traditional relationships. From princes falling in love with women of different classes and races, to women in power falling in love with the men committed to serving them, V. Vee is sure to live up to the creed: Mixing sexiness, romance, and equality to create true love.

A single parent, disabled veteran, and a child of veterans, V. Vee has lived all over the US nation, and even Cuba, but dreams of one day returning to either New York or California…if Boston doesn't work out. Any place is fine as long as it's not Florida. V. Vee loves to hear from readers and is completely open to hearing about the single brother you have who may be bisexual, or gay, or the family member who is trans, or a veteran, or how you want to be an author someday. Just be sure to label the email appropriately, it's embarrassing to offer writing advice to potential husbands.

Really. It is.

Website: http://vveetheauthor.wordpress.com

Twitter: http://www.twitter.com/VVeeB

Facebook: http://www.facebook.com/VVeeVAlex

http://facebook.com/AuthorVVee

Instagram: http://www.instagram.com/vveeauthor

Email: authorvvee@gmail.com

🍬 🍬 🍬 🍬

The Bad Boy Princes Of

Malvidence

A Royal Secret

The Royal Nanny

The Royal Beauty

The Royal Diva (Coming Soon)

Woodland Pack

Growl's Queen: The Full Novel

Howl's Beauty (Coming Soon)

Wedding Crashing

Her Wedding

Their Wedding (Coming Soon)

Athlete's Wives

Perfectly Crazy (Prequel)

Balls & Booties (Coming Soon)

For The Love Of The Irish

The Mad Kitty (Prequel)

The Irishman

Kyra: The Irishman's Wife (Coming Soon)

Nia: The Irishman's Sister (Coming Soon)

Galvin: The Irishman's Brother (Coming Soon)

Malvidencian Royals

A French Romance

The Royal Baker (Found in The Royal Court Anthology)

Loving An Officer

Cuffed and Unashamed (Coming Soon)

Lingerie

Say Yes (Coming Sept 2020)

NY Vampires

Bound (Coming April 2020)

Rachel & Ryan

35/F Seeks Alpha

38/F Seeks Happily Ever After

(Coming November 2020)

For The Love Of The Marines

Luca (Coming Soon)

Devil (Coming Soon)

Standalones

Bellissima Donna Crudele (Once Upon A Villain, 10)

Nikki & Tommy's Enchantment (Coming Soon)

One For My Baby (Coming Soon)

From Leyah (Dark Romance Pen Name):

Burn The World Down Book 1

Burn The World Down Book 2 (Coming Soon)

Burn The World Down Book 3 (Coming Soon)

Blood On Their Hands (Coming Soon)

A chance meeting in the park leads to a hilarious romance.

One For My Baby

USA TODAY Bestselling Author
V. Vee

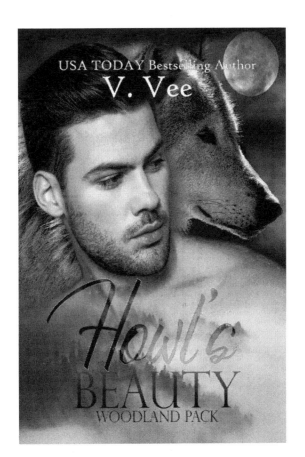

A Dark Vampire Romance

NY Vampires

USA TODAY Bestselling Author
V. Vee

IF ANYONE KNEW MY SECRET, I WOULD BE KILLED. IF
THEY KNEW ABOUT HIM, THEY WOULD MAKE IT
SLOW.

I AM
COMMAND

A FELINE ASSASSINS NOVELLA

USA TODAY Bestselling Author
V. Vee

THIS IS NOT A ROMANCE
I BELONG TO HIM.
WHETHER I WANT TO OR NOT.
YOU BELONG TO ME
AN EROTIC THRILLER
V. A. BAILEY

"Warning: This book contains graphic material that may be disturbing for some readers."

Shattered

She was shattered from the events of one night.
But now it was time to fight back.

International Bestselling Author V. Vee as

V. A. Bailey

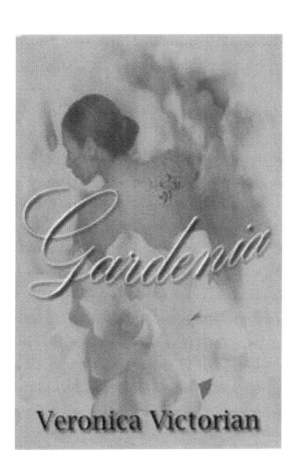

Gardenia

Veronica Victorian

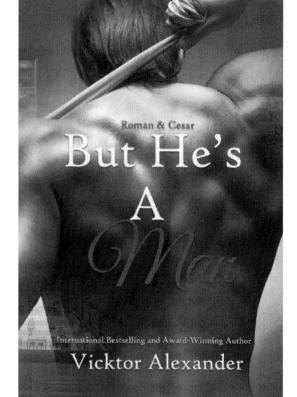

Roman & Cesar

But He's
A
Man

International Bestselling and Award-Winning Author

Vicktor Alexander

Made in the USA
Columbia, SC
08 January 2020